PIE IN THE SKY

WENDY MASS

Little, Brown and Company

New York Boston

Copyright © 2013 by Wendy Mass
Interior illustrations by Lauren Gentry/Jelly London
Excerpt from *Every Soul a Star* copyright © 2008 by Wendy Mass
Reader's Guide copyright © 2013 by Hachette Book Group, Inc.
Pi in the Sky Reader's Guide prepared by Jennifer McMahon

Little, Brown and Company

Hachette Book Group
1290 Avenue of the Americas, New York, NY 10104
Visit our website at lb-kids.com

Little, Brown and Company is a division of Hachette Book Group, Inc.
The Little, Brown name and logo are trademarks of Hachette Book Group, Inc.

The publisher is not responsible for websites (or their content)
that are not owned by the publisher.

First Paperback Edition: April 2014
First published in hardcover in June 2013 by Little, Brown and Company

Library of Congress Cataloging-in-Publication Data

Mass, Wendy, 1967–
  Pi in the sky / Wendy Mass. — First edition.
     pages cm
  Summary: Joss, the seventh son of the Supreme Overlord of the Universe, must team up with a human girl to re-create Earth, when the planet is accidentally erased from existence.
  ISBN 978-0-316-08916-6 (hc) — ISBN 978-0-316-08917-3 (pb)
  [1. Universe—Fiction. 2. Earth—Fiction. 3. Science fiction.] I. Title.
II. Title: Pie in the sky.
  PZ7.M42355Pi 2009
  [Fic]—dc23   2012030638

10 9 8 7

LSC-C

Printed in the United States of America

For my son Griffin, who loves to ask questions about the universe. May the stars continue to shine through you, all the days of your life.

* ✳ *

And in memory of the great astronomer Carl Sagan, who taught a generation not only to wonder at the universe, but to seek to understand it. He inspired the scientific leaders of today to carry on that task, many of whose words shape this story.

"Penetrating so many secrets, we cease to believe in the unknowable. But there it sits nevertheless, calmly licking its chops."

— H. L. Mencken, journalist

"If the atoms that make up the world around us could tell their stories, each and every one of them would sing a tale to dwarf the greatest epics of literature."

— Marcus Chown, physicist

* * * * * *

WHAT YOU NEED TO KNOW

* * * * * *

O kay, first off, the quotes that start each chapter are from real people who know a lot of really cool things. You'll probably recognize some of their names. Second, you should know that this story takes place completely in The Realms (pronounced like relms, not reelms, which would just be weird). What are The Realms, you ask? *Where* are The Realms? Well, those are tricky questions. I have a theory, but it's a guess, at best, and I hope you won't hold me to it. Come closer and I'll tell you.

The Realms aren't so much *somewhere* as they are *everywhere*. And to explain *that*, I'll need to start by explaining the discovery of a mysterious substance called dark matter.

Hang in there now. This won't hurt a bit.

Basically, a lot of supersmart scientists who have spent a REALLY LONG TIME in school tell us that most of the "stuff" in our universe (96 percent) is invisible. Even though dark matter is all around us, we can't see it. Not even with the help of those enormous telescopes that see so far out into space that they are really seeing back in time.

And why can't we see dark matter? Well, those same smart scientists will tell you it's because dark matter doesn't give off, or reflect, or absorb any light that we can see or measure. But we know it's there because it attracts regular matter, the stuff we CAN see. Dark matter allows gravity to spin gas and dust into stars and planets and galaxies. It gives structure to the cosmos, like the scaffolding of a building.

Yes, that's what your science teacher would tell you. But that's hardly the whole story. The real reason we can't see dark matter is because that's where The Realms are located and they have EXCELLENT cloaking devices. Truly, the universe is a much stranger place than most people give it credit for, teeming with life and full of secrets.

Now you might be wondering what goes on in The Realms. And what this has to do with us, tucked away on our comfortable little planet, a safe twenty-seven thousand light-years away from the massive black hole asleep at the center of our Milky Way Galaxy. Well, who better to answer those questions than someone who has lived in The Realms his whole life? Someone around your age, with the same kinds of dreams, desires, and hopes for the future. Someone who thinks that nothing very exciting happens in his life. He doesn't know it yet, but that's about to change. So sit back, relax, and enjoy. Because in about seven pages, the gravity that keeps your feet glued to the ground will be gone.

Don't say I didn't warn you.

If you wish to make an apple pie from scratch, you must first invent the universe.

—**Carl Sagan, astronomer**

1

If you think it's tough being the Supreme Overlord of the Universe, try being his son.

Or, more precisely, his *seventh* son. That whole thing about the seventh son being special in some way? Just a rumor spread by a few disgruntled seventh sons trying to make a name for themselves. In my experience, being the seventh son only means that by the time I got here, my brothers had taken all the cool gigs. They spend their days creating new species, choreographing sunrises and sunsets, composing the music of the spheres by keeping planets in their orbits, inspiring great artists, overseeing the Afterlives, and testing new, state-of-the-art video games on the planets whose inhabitants haven't yet discovered how to access most of their brain cells. Me? I deliver pies.

That's right. I. Deliver. *Pies.*

Cherry pies. Apple pies. Strawberry-rhubarb pies. True, my pies happen to be the glue that holds the very fabric of the universe together, but have no illusion—they are still pies. I guess you could say they're pretty *big* pies, but size—like time—is relative. To a creature living on one of the millions of inhabited planets that it is our job to oversee, the pies might be as big as a moon or as small as, well, a pie. Hard to say for sure, since I've never been out of The Realms. But that's a whole other gripe.

The point is, a long time ago, the Powers That Be (known simply as the PTB) decided it was getting messy trying to control the forces that keep the stars and planets and galaxies from crashing into each other. So they decided to combine the fundamental forces of nature and somehow shape them into a nice, sweet-smelling pie. Why a pie? Why *not* a pie! Who doesn't like pie?

It's my job to pick up the pies fresh from the oven, box them up, and deliver them to the correct department at the Powers That Be headquarters, which currently looks like a giant boot but can change regularly.

Anyway, when I pick up the empty pie tins at the end of my shift, only crumbs are left. Somehow the Powers That Be distribute the pies to the far reaches of the universe, wherever new star systems are forming. Since the universe is constantly expanding, this means my job is never done. I don't actually know the nitty-gritty of what happens to the pies once they reach their destinations, which is unfortunate because I have this big report due for school next week on what my job entails, and that's the kind of detail teachers eat right up.

Yes, even immortal sons of Supreme Overlords have to go to school, which doesn't really seem fair. I mean, I might have only begun my teen years, but years here last *forever*, so really, I've been in school since before the Sombrero Galaxy took its first siesta billions of years ago. It's enough already.

Anyway, right now I'm heading to my last pickup of the day and then I have to go home and write the annoying report. At least the pickup is at my best friend Kal's house. Kal's parents are OnWorlders, which means they live most of the time on different terrestrial planets, doing research and writing reports. As a rule, we never interfere with the planets' natural evolution. That said, I've heard rumors. After all, there's only so much one can take of watching dinosaurs stomp around aimlessly for a few hundred million years before you need to send an asteroid their way.

No matter how many times I walk this same path, I never get bored of it. The central Realms—home to most of the residents and buildings—are set up like a grid, with walking paths crisscrossing each other at even intervals. On either side of the paths trees loom high and streams weave their way between them. When I was younger, before I started delivering the pies, I could usually be found in one of the distant fields with Kal or Bren, watching the clouds change color. The sky here is without color, but the clouds more than make up for it. I learned in school that on the planets, clouds and trees and water are solid objects, providing some sort of purpose in nature. In The Realms, they are more like *suggestions* of such things, until someone wants to use them. A lake becomes a lake when someone wants to go fishing. A flower becomes a flower when someone wants to water it, or admire it, or put it in a vase. Even then it's not a "real" flower, like the type that grows in the soil of many of the terrestrial planets. But that doesn't make it any less beautiful.

Aunt Rae's front lawn is full of flowers growing from nowhere and rootless trees. She's very proud of her garden, and when she's not making pies, I usually find her gardening out here.

"Took you long enough," Kal says, swinging the door open. Kal—whose after-school job is to welcome new arrivals to the Afterlives—has a greater sense of time than most of us here in The Realms. Since he deals with life-forms whose lives actually *have* beginnings and endings, the whole thing sort of rubs off on him and he gets impatient easily.

I plop down on the couch and say, "I'm here the same time I always am."

He mutters something that I choose to ignore. I put up my feet and breathe in deep. Their house smells soooo good. Aunt Rae is one of the best pie makers in all The Realms, but she is also the slowest. *Can't rush perfection* is her motto. I never mind waiting. Any time I get to put my feet up and do nothing works fine for me.

"Is that you, Joss?" Aunt Rae calls out from the kitchen. She always knows when I'm here, even though she's nearly completely deaf. She sticks her head out from the kitchen, apple pie juice running down the front of her apron.

"Hi, Aunt Rae," I yell. "How are you today?"

Kal's aunt is one of the Old Ones. All the pie makers are from the first wave of immortals. It's not like their bodies are breaking down or anything, but they don't self-repair as well as the rest of us. Of course, Aunt Rae could get her hearing fixed instantly instead of wearing an adjustable ear volumizer, but she says the silence helps her focus on baking her pies. Personally, I think she likes not having to hear Kal's music blaring all the time. He has terrible taste in music, even with all the music in the universe to choose from. He's been working on his own "masterpiece," which is even worse.

"Can't complain," Aunt Rae replies cheerily, wiping her forehead and leaving a smear of flour behind.

"Wanna hear my latest and greatest?" Kal asks me, picking up his drumsticks without waiting for an answer.

Aunt Rae switches her volumizer to the *off* position and ducks back into the kitchen. I cover my ears with my hands. As usual, this is the point where I get even *more* jealous that my oldest brother, Thade, gets to hear the Music of the Spheres—that melodic tune made by the planetary bodies as they go around their orbits—while I get to hear Kal doing things to the drums that should never, ever be described as music. Kal claims he learned this latest piece from a drummer in a band he recently escorted to the Afterlives. The guy had come from Earth, which is a particularly well-liked planet around here due to its being one of the few where the inhabitants developed a sense of humor.

It's only when Kal pauses to flip his drumsticks dramatically in the air that we hear the sirens. He drops the drumsticks, and one hits the cymbal with a *tszing*! The sirens mean only one thing—someone on one of the inhabited planets is zeroing in on our location with whatever technology they've developed to peer into their night sky. Normally, The Realms can't be seen from anywhere in the universe. But every once in a while a rip occurs in the fabric of the space-time continuum. Quantum entanglement becomes untangled. If someone happened to be looking at exactly the right spot, they could catch a glimpse of us. And just the tiniest glimpse is catastrophic.

I was only a billion or two years old, a baby really, when the sirens last blared. Intelligent life in the first batch of planets had just started peering into the skies. The viewer at the other end of the primitive piece of equipment spotted a garden party at one of the fancier estates in The Realms. The old guy was so shocked at what he saw that he dropped dead of a heart attack on the spot. Dying in this way was actually a bit of luck for everyone else on his planet, since the penalty for laying eyes on any of the beings living in The Realms is the immediate disintegration of the entire planet. Under the circumstances, in an uncharacteristically charitable move, the Powers That Be allowed the planet to continue existing. *A dead man tells no tales*, as the saying goes. But I doubt they will be so forgiving again. No one knows exactly why the punishment is so harsh, but since this almost never happens, the whole issue doesn't get much attention.

"DUCK!" Kal screams, throwing himself to the floor. Between the intermittent wails of the siren, I can still hear Aunt Rae humming.

"Aunt Rae!" I yell. "You have to duck!"

But she doesn't hear me. Even the sirens don't get through when her volumizer is off.

I half-slither, half-crawl on my elbows and knees to the opening of the kitchen. Kal follows close on my heels. Aunt Rae is reaching into the oven, pulling out a perfect, steaming-hot apple pie. I reach up to grab the hem of her apron just as she turns around.

But I'm too late. The area around her vibrates and shudders, almost imperceptibly, then settles back into place. No doubt about it, she has been spotted. Someone has broken (or at least bent really far) the laws of physics and has laid eyes on Aunt Rae and her famous apple pie. It is the last thing he will ever see. He will not get the chance to tell anyone on his planet of his discovery. There will no longer be anyone to tell.

The wail of the siren now becomes one long keening cry. No one likes to think of any of the worlds ending. We've watched them grow from grains of dust, so it's quite heart-breaking. The siren fades out. I roll over onto my back and stare up at the ceiling.

"Joss?" Aunt Rae asks, leaning over me with obvious concern. She flips her volumizer back on. "What is it?"

But I can only shake my head, a tear sliding down my nose. I know new planets are being formed constantly, new civilizations rising and falling and rising again, but still, it's a huge loss.

"I hope it wasn't Earth," Kal says, his expression grim.

I nod in agreement. Besides the fact that the people of Earth understand that flatulence can be funny, they have the tastiest enchiladas. Actually, those two things are most likely connected. While there are millions of planets in the universe with some form of life, they are all in vastly differ-ent stages of development and intelligence. Many never develop technology at all, never learn how to harness the elements and forces around them. But if they do, and if they can't control it, they usually destroy themselves pretty soon after. This leaves only a narrow window when the inhabit-ants are using their knowledge to educate themselves, to look out at the universe and seek answers. Earth is in this zone right now.

A voice booms through the house. "Joss! Are you still there?"

I jump up from the floor so quickly my brain spins. Kal and I stare at each other. My father NEVER uses the communication network himself. As Supreme Overlord, he has a whole staff for that. The fact that he is calling me now can't be a good sign.

"Answer him," Kal hisses.

I clear my throat. "Yes, Dad, I'm here."

"Report immediately to PTB headquarters."

"Yes, sir," I reply, halfway out of the kitchen.

But he isn't finished. "And bring the pie!"

2

I weave my way in and out of the busy streets, the steaming pie tin burning my hands. I hadn't even given Aunt Rae a chance to put it in a box. As always, when I first picked up the pie, I felt a sort of current go through me, like my body was getting heavier. It must be something in the pies that causes it. The feeling is not entirely unpleasant, and I like to linger before it fades. But I couldn't do that this time. As relative as time is in The Realms, my father does not like to be kept waiting. And when he does not like something, you do your best to avoid it.

The streets are usually not this crowded. With so much space in The Realms, there is rarely a reason for people to gather. But the blare of the sirens got everyone out and talking. I push through a group of kids I go to school with, which is made easier by the fact that they part slightly when they see me coming. This is one of the downsides to having a really important father—the other kids keep their distance from me. All except Kal, who I can always count on to remind me that I may have a famous family, but my hair grows in lopsided and no girl has ever gone on a date with me twice.

In the olden days, we used to be able to travel instantaneously, winking in and out of places like the smallest of elementary particles. Those were the days. Everything was so easy then. Took me a tenth of the time to complete my daily pie-delivering, leaving endless opportunities to clown around with Kal or bowl down at Thunder Lanes. But the Powers That Be fixed it so our bodies can no longer vibrate at a high-enough frequency to achieve this state. We also feel pain now, which is bothersome. They decided we needed to live more like our mortal kinsmen in order to better serve their needs. The PTB are strange that way. Their main job is to oversee the various species who populate the universe, but a lot of the time they seem not to care much. Suns explode in fiery supernovas, wiping out any life-forms unfortunate enough to be within fifty light-years, sending their atoms spewing forth into the void of space, and do the PTB do anything to stop it?

No. No, they do not.

Civilizations destroy themselves (and others) over and over again, and the PTB watch on the planet view screens and place bets on what the last survivor's final words will be. (They're usually something like, "Oh, crud.") This is not quite as cruel as it sounds, since the bylaws of the Powers That Be strictly forbid interfering or choosing sides in planetary squabbles. This is widely agreed to be the best course of action. Might they turn their backs occasionally and allow someone to steer a meteorite embedded with amino acids toward a recently cooled planet in a new solar system? Sure. Prevent nuclear destruction of an advanced civilization? No.

"I'm coming with you," Kal calls out, catching up to me on the street. Kal has transformed his legs into wheels, which was very smart of him. Even though all of us in The Realms can quickly rearrange the cells in our bodies to create new patterns, I usually don't think of it. It takes a lot of mental effort, and I prefer to save that effort for school so I don't fail out. Plus, with wheels, you wind up with all sorts of bruises, and you have to pick pieces of dirt and random tiny objects from your skin long after you've turned them back into legs.

"You should go home, Kal. My dad didn't sound happy. You don't want to be around when he's not happy. Remember that time he turned you into a cow pie because you wouldn't stop drumming with your fork and spoon when you came over for dinner?"

Kal shudders at the smelly memory but squares his shoulders and says, "It was my fault we didn't hear the sirens sooner. You shouldn't have to take the blame."

"I wasn't going to," I reply. I'm lying and we both know it. I've been taking the fall for Kal since we were in diapers. As a son of the Supreme Overlord, I do get special treatment. The PTB often look the other way if one of my brothers or I bend the rules every now and then. Bren (the brother closest to my age and the one I like the best) and I once broke into the Department of Gravity to see if we could find some gravitons to take us to a neighboring universe. We'd heard rumors of other universes that waves of gravity could travel between. It didn't matter to us that in billions of years no one had ever found these universes, supposedly full of their own stars and planets and galaxies. We got caught, of course, because there's no way to sneak around here without everyone knowing your business.

Since everyone's afraid of our father, all *we* got was a warning. (The next person who got caught breaking in there was turned into an ear mite. He was last seen living inside the ear of a particularly smelly Plumpadorus in the Cygnus Galaxy.) But what happened today will likely result in more than a slap on the wrist and a lecture.

Kal and I come to a stop in front of PTB headquarters. No longer a giant boot, the building has been transformed into a flagpole, with a black flag flying at half-mast in honor of the recently destroyed planet.

The shape of the building makes it so we have to enter single file. Kal converts his wheels back to legs, and we hurry up the elevator to the inner sanctum of the PTB. After recent events, I expect to find the place a madhouse, with committee members running to and fro, arms full of reports to file. If nothing else, the department that oversees the Afterlives must surely be gearing up for an extremely busy afternoon. Instead, the place has a quiet hush to it.

The few people I do see are speaking in whispers. Kal and I exchange a worried look.

The door to my father's office swings open to reveal the top members of the Powers That Be gathered around the huge round table, grim expressions on their faces. I notice that half of them are wearing their ceremonial robes, and are all men. If I had to guess, the female leaders were not happy with the decision to destroy the planet and stormed out in protest. My mother—an honorary member due to marrying my father—reports this happens fairly regularly.

My father glances away from the holographic view screen hovering slightly above his head. An odd look crosses his face when he sees Kal beside me. Dad's not a huge fan. He doesn't think Kal has enough "drive." Kal actually has plenty of drive. It's just usually not in the right direction.

My father waves us in. "I'm glad Kal's here."

Kal's face pales and I shiver involuntarily. My father is never glad to see Kal.

I place the pie on the table, where it sits, ignored. "Don't blame Kal, Dad. It's my fault we didn't get to warn Aunt Rae in time."

"This isn't about placing blame," Dad says. "We have a much bigger issue to deal with."

"That's a relief," Kal says, color returning to his cheeks.

"Not really," one of the suited men around the table mutters. I can never tell the suited guys apart. Well, that's not really true. I've never actually tried. This one—short, with green hair—hands Kal a holographic screen that hovers in his palm. "We saved this for you," he says.

"For me?" Kal asks. "Why? What is it?"

"It is a log of your parents' last report," the green-haired guy replies. "They sent it only two days ago from a planet in the Milky Way Galaxy. From Earth. We assume they haven't left the planet."

Kal gives the report a quick glance. "They go to Earth pretty regularly. Am I missing something?"

"I'm sorry, Kal," my father says, when no one else replies. "We had no choice. Earth is gone."

3

deafening silence fills the room as everyone
watches Kal. As virtually immortal life-forms,
we don't have to breathe unless we want to,
and at this moment no one is.

My hand on his shoulder, I can feel Kal trembling. His
knees are locked in place, which is probably the only thing
keeping him standing. He refuses to turn away from the
transparent wall of my father's office. We are high up in
The Realms here, with the whole universe spread out
around us. Usually the sight of billions of galaxies swirling
like glittering diamonds is mesmerizing. Today, though, we
cannot see its beauty. Today the distant clusters of stars only
serve to remind us how, in a universe teeming with energy
and drama, one small planet in the Orion Arm of the Milky
Way barely counts for anything (no matter how much fun
it is to watch their football games on our view screens).

We have been raised to believe that in the grand scheme of things, one planet doesn't matter. *Can't* matter.

Unless your best friend's parents are on it when it's destroyed.

"But I don't understand," Kal says, his voice sadder than I've ever heard it. (And I've heard him sing the blues—badly, but he's sung them.) "My parents are immortal, like all of us. Wouldn't they have survived the destruction of Earth?"

"That was our assumption, too," my father says. "But we have not found any trace of them."

Kal still won't turn away from the window. It's like he's searching the vastness of space for some sign of his parents. Through gritted teeth, he asks, "Did you know they were there? Before?"

"Of course not," says my father's second-in-command, striding into the room. His name is Gluck the Yuck, a nickname my brothers and I gave him because he refuses to rearrange his facial features to be even the slightest bit pleasing. He's not a bad guy, just a little hard to look at.

"Well, we didn't exactly *check*," admits the green-haired suit. I really should learn their names.

"There wasn't time to check," insists another. "The destruction has to be instantaneous. And what would be the odds of your parents working on that particular planet at the exact time someone from there would view The Realms? The odds are astronomical, that's what they are."

A nice try to deflect blame, but we all know that the odds

of anything existing in the universe at all is astronomical, so the man's argument falls short.

"I know!" Kal exclaims, whirling around to face the PTB. "The Afterlives will be flooded with all the new arrivals. I'm sure I'll be called into work. My parents will still show up there with all the Earth people, right? So they'll be back after all!"

The committee members exchange uneasy glances. They look to Gluck to reply. Gluck then looks pointedly at my father. For the first time in my (very long) memory, my father hesitates before answering. "No one will be coming to the Afterlives."

Kal scrunches his brows. "I don't understand. There were billions of people on that planet."

Dad looks uncomfortable, which is not a good look on the Supreme Overlord of the Universe. "We didn't exactly destroy the planet. Per se."

"So my parents are still alive!" Kal shouts. He grabs my father's arm, then immediately lets go when my father glares down at him. In a less shouty voice Kal asks, "Why did you say they're gone?"

My father sighs. "Perhaps I should have chosen my words more carefully. If someone never existed, you couldn't truly say they were gone, could you?"

This is as good a time as any to admit that I'm only the sixth smartest of Dad's seven sons. My brother Laz is generally considered the least smart, at least when it comes to school stuff. He fails Planet Building class every term. He's always calculating pi wrong, so his planets keep straying from their orbits and crashing into everyone else's. But even with my limited brainpower, I can tell my father isn't making any sense. "Dad, what are you trying to say?"

He sits back down at the head of the table and places his large hands on the gleaming surface. The holograph pops back up. He pushes it toward Kal and me. All I see is a dark blob.

"The last time The Realms were spotted," my father says, "the spotter's planet was able to escape harm due to his being thoughtful enough to die on the spot."

"Yes, we all know that," I say, anxious for him to get to the point.

"And the time before that," he continues, "the planet was far from its sun, leading to very harsh living conditions. Only a few species had evolved, and their numbers stayed small. It was fairly easy to log them into the Afterlives in an orderly fashion. But in the case of Earth, which supported such an abundance of life..." He trails off, clears his throat, and continues. "Basically, the Afterlives would have been totally overwhelmed, so the PTB came up with a better idea." He pauses and glances at Gluck, who nods his encouragement. Dad sighs. "We ripped Earth out of the space-time continuum."

Kal repeats the words, but slower. "You ripped Earth... out of space-time?"

"Technically we couldn't just take Earth," Gluck explains, "since it's gravitationally bound up with the sun and the rest of the solar system...."

"So we took that, too," Green-Haired Suit continues.

"You took their *sun*?" I ask, hoping I heard him wrong.

Green-Haired Suit nods. One of the PTB wearing a long white robe centuries out of style adds, "And the rest of the planets. And their moons and the asteroids and comets and such."

I clutch the back of a nearby chair to steady myself. From all my years of history class, I know nothing like this ever happened before. To interfere in the universe on such a grand scale is just unheard of. Kal, too, is frozen from the shock of it.

"We didn't have much choice, Joss," my father says. "None of our options were good. If we had exploded the planet, gravity from the sun would have kept the pieces grouped together. A dead world, clinging to chunks of life-less rock. No one wants to see that."

I shudder.

Dad puts his large, steady hand on my shoulder. "Or if we simply took away the sun, Earth would have gone shoot-ing off into space, and a rogue planet aimlessly hurtling about is simply too dangerous. We considered halting the planet's rotation, but what a mess that would make, since everything on the surface would keep moving. This way it's nice and neat, and we don't have that nag-ging guilt at killing off a five-billion-year-old planet. Now Earth never actually existed, so no one had to die. It's a plan we've had in place for a while, in case the occasion ever arose."

Kal makes a sound that falls somewhere between a whimper and a growl. He faces my father and says, "According to your logic, my parents never existed, since they were ripped right out of time, too, right?"

"I suppose you could say that, unfortunately. Yes."

Kal puts his hands on his hips. "Then why am *I* still here?"

I turn to Dad to await his answer. We all know about cause and effect. It's one of the basic laws of the universe. The arrow of time goes in one direction only. First comes *cause*, then *effect*. Even *I* know you can't have a kid without having his parents first.

But Dad only stares at Kal. Or should I say, stares at the spot where Kal had been standing. For Kal, my best friend, my childhood companion in all things, is totally, utterly gone. Gone like back in the days when we were able to wink in and out of places, but those days are far in the past. Is he hiding behind a chair? I peer under the table, but all I see are a lot of hairy legs in sensible shoes.

He's just . . . gone.

"Hmm," Gluck says thoughtfully. "I was afraid that might happen."

Before I can question them on Kal's sudden and utter disappearance, he's made MORE gone by the fact that in his place now stands a tall, skinny girl wearing a big red parka, a white ski hat, and a sour expression.

"Fascinating!" exclaims my father.

"Now *that*," says Gluck, "I didn't see coming."

Any sufficiently advanced technology is indistinguishable from magic.

—Arthur C. Clarke, writer

Seriously?" the girl says, looking around the room in annoyance. "First I dream about some old lady baking a pie, and now this? I totally shouldn't have watched that *Star Trek* marathon last weekend. My father's never going to let me forget it if I sleep through the closest approach of Mars in like, sixty thousand years. He'll keep dragging me outside in the middle of the night, pointing his new telescope at the sky until I go off to college." She starts pinching her arm. "Why am I not waking up?"

The PTB stare at one another in amazement, and it takes a lot to amaze these guys.

"Fascinating!" Dad repeats, beaming. He loves the mysterious and unexplainable. That's why he's so good at his job.

I just gape.

Dad walks over to the girl and touches her on the arm. They both jump back.

"So solid!" Dad exclaims. "Gluck, you have to feel this!"

Gluck makes a move toward the girl, but I step in front of him. "Wait! You can't just go around feeling people's arms."

"That's right," she says, with only a cursory glance my way. "Don't you people have any manners?" Then, surprisingly, she laughs and shakes her head. "Look at me, talking to people in my own dream. What are you supposed to do in nightmares again? Oh, right." She turns to my father and shouts, "Be gone, freaky dream guy. And your freaky dream friends, too!" Then in her regular voice she says, "But I like the green hair, dude. It's a good look for you." She turns to Gluck and shudders. "How did I dream *you* up? You look like your face got caught in a garbage disposal!"

If I weren't so traumatized by Kal's disappearance I would chuckle at that one.

A few of the PTB rush from their seats. "You cannot talk that way to the Supreme Overlord of the Universe and the Powers That Be!" they bellow. "You are in the presence of greatness!"

The girl quickly steps back until she is inches away from the invisible wall that overlooks the cosmos. My father holds up his hand. "It is all right, gentlemen. She means no harm."

She looks like she doesn't know *what* she means right

now. Her brows are furrowed in confusion. Fear alternates with indignant determination. She yanks off her hat and stuffs it into a coat pocket. She then crosses her arms in front of her. Or tries to, but her parka is so puffy her arms get stuck trying to get around her elbows. With a grunt of frustration, she unzips the coat, throws it on the floor, and begins stomping on it.

While she's distracted with that, my father nudges me and whispers, "Go talk to her. You two look about the same age, so she won't perceive you as a threat."

"But what about Kal?" I whisper back. "We need to find out what happened to him and how to get him back. We have to hurry."

"We'll talk about the Kal situation later, I promise." He nudges me again. "Go. And ask her how she got here."

But I can't seem to move. Kal is not a "situation." He's my best friend. The only person outside my family I really trust. I'm not even sure I trust everyone *inside* my family, actually. Kal is the person who understands me the best. And he's gone. GONE. Things like this—shocking, unexpected things—don't happen here. The universe might be a seething, swirling, booming place. But after nearly fourteen billion years of the same sorts of things happening—a sun exploding here, a galaxy colliding there, a new species sprouting up on a new planet—life in The Realms has fallen into a sort of "been there, done that" kind of routine. I admit, I like it this way. Unlike my father, I am not at all fascinated by the unexpected. At least not when it involves losing my best friend and one of my favorite planets.

"Joss!" my dad booms. I startle and turn my attention back to the girl, who is still stomping on her coat.

After one last jump-stomp combination with her clunky black boots, she kicks the coat, and it lands a foot away from me. Aware that my father's eyes are on my back, I bend down to pick it up. Moving slowly so as not to frighten or anger her, I hold out her coat. "You really don't like this parka, do you?"

She looks at it but doesn't take it. "It's puffy and red and stupid and I hate it. Plus, it makes me look twelve years old."

"How old *are* you?"

She shrugs. "Twelve."

When I can't think of a suitable reply, she adds, "But I'll be thirteen really soon."

"I just turned thirteen," I say. It's more like a few *billion* and thirteen, but she probably doesn't want to hear that. "So . . . how did you, uh, get here?"

Ignoring my question, she steps closer to me, examining my face carefully. "You have really perfect skin, anyone ever tell you that? Like, no pores. My friend Lydia is obsessed with her pores and spends hours in front of her magnifying mirror. She'd hate you."

"That's nice to know," I say, not really sure what pores are. To be polite, I say, "My name's Joss. What's your name?"

"Annika Klutzman," she replies, then glances down at

her watch. I'm shocked to see the second hand ticking the time away. Eyebrows rise all around the room. Time is measured by how long it takes a planet to revolve around its sun, and we have no sun. Her watch should not work in The Realms.

"I really need to go," she says, blinking fast. "This is the LONGEST dream, and I've got to wake up. I don't want to sleep the night away and miss the whole Mars approach. Well, I *do* want to miss it, but it's important to my dad, so . . ." She starts pinching her arm again. Then she squeezes her eyes closed and open, closed and open. She takes a big gulp of air (we don't have oxygen here, which begs the question of how she can breathe), holds it, then lets it out. "Ugh," she says. "I'm still here."

My father taps his large foot impatiently.

I repeat my previous question. "So, um, how did you get here again?"

"Honestly," she says, "I don't really remember falling asleep. One minute I'm looking through Dad's scope at the sky where, as usual, nothing is happening, and then I must have fallen asleep because suddenly I see this old lady with flour on her face, pulling a pie out of an oven." She pauses. "I think it was apple."

"And then you were here, in my father's office?"

She nods. "Pretty much. That dream faded into dark and then this one started. You know how dreams are."

I don't, actually, since we don't dream here. We don't

sleep much, either, maybe once every few months. But I nod politely.

She looks around again, clearly trying to make sense of her surroundings. I try to see PTB headquarters through her eyes, with her limited senses. Like the rest of the universe, The Realms are made of concentrated energy disguised as matter. But in the rest of the universe, all the matter—all the *stuff*—is made of tiny dancing particles inside only slightly larger atoms. And except for hydrogen, almost all those atoms, including the ones that make up her own body, were forged inside exploding stars. Here in The Realms, those tiny particles aren't so tiny. Humans are made of trillions and trillions of atoms, of all different elements. We are made of only a hundred atoms and only primordial elements, the ones that were here at the very beginning of space and time, the ones that no other beings in the universe can see. We are more gas than solid, more energy than matter. Our surroundings shimmer and glow, vibrate and pulse. Sounds weird, but you get used to it.

As for the people, the inhabitants of The Realms mostly look like the kind of people she's used to. We have brains and hearts and skin like most of the species in the universe, but we are very different from them. Basically, we are only a bit denser than our surroundings. Like a liquid on Earth, we can mold ourselves to fit any container. Last century it was very trendy to take the shape of Blopies, the purple blobs from a planet with a really weak gravitational force in the Whirlpool Galaxy. The Blopie craze died out when people missed having hands.

I'm suddenly not sure how much I'm supposed to say to this girl, this living, breathing human. Do I tell her she's in The Realms, and that this isn't a dream? Do I explain that the PTB made it so her entire solar system never actually existed? All because of her? I want to ask about Kal, but it's all too much to process. I glance at Dad for help.

"Permit me to explain," he says, stepping closer to us. The girl flinches but holds her ground.

"I am Joss's father, and you could say I run this place."

No longer hindered by her huge coat, Annika crosses her arms successfully this time. "No disrespect, mister, but you don't run my dream."

A flash of anger crosses my father's face, but it is gone so quickly that her senses wouldn't have noticed even a flicker in his expression.

"You are right, of course," he says. "I will defer to your nocturnal flights of fancy."

"Good," she says. "Whatever that means. Well, since this dream won't seem to go away on its own, I'm gonna curl up and ignore it till it does. So . . . see ya." She takes her coat from my hands, drops it to the floor, then lies down on top of it and closes her eyes. Instantly, gentle snores fill the cavernous room.

Dad and I share a surprised glance. The PTB grumble angrily. Really, no inhabitant of The Realms would EVER treat my dad this way. But Dad motions all of us to the other side of the room.

"Let her be for now," he says. "Joss, you wait here until she's ready to talk again."

The PTB hurry out, probably glad to be released of any responsibility for the strange girl. Gluck the Yuck is the only one who stays with us.

"Dad, you promised to get Kal back."

He glances at Gluck before answering. "It's not that easy."

"You've been saying that a lot today. *Everything's* easy for you. You're the Supreme Overlord of the Universe!"

"True," he admits. "But I still have to abide by the same fundamental laws of nature as everyone else."

Gluck puts his hand on my arm. "Listen, Joss. What happened to Kal is very straightforward. As the arrow of time sped backward, his parents got younger and younger. As the billions of years wound down, and the last of their essence was lost, Kal was lost, too."

I turn to Dad for verification of this. He nods. "I'm sorry, son, but look on the bright side. Kal doesn't know he's gone, so he's not suffering." He gestures over to the sleeping girl. "And now you have a new companion. She seems...nice."

"And she has a lot of spunk," adds Gluck.

I know they're just trying to be helpful, but do they really think Kal, who was supposed to be my sidekick for the rest of eternity, can be replaced by a strange girl from a terrestrial planet who hates red parkas and will live no longer than a few billion heartbeats? I shake my head. "Gluck has pimples that have longer life spans than her."

"Now that's just rude," Dad scolds.

"I'll let it go," Gluck says, "since you're obviously upset."

"How can she even BE here?" I ask. "We don't have an atmosphere like Earth's at all. No oxygen or sunlight or any of the things she needs to live."

Dad shrugs. "And yet she lives."

"For now, anyway," Gluck adds.

"What's that supposed to mean?"

"You saw how easily she fell asleep."

"So?"

"Never mind that now," my father says. "We have more important things to worry about than her sleeping habits. We have a living human in The Realms for the first time in the history of the universe. This is exactly why the consequences for viewing The Realms are so swift and dire. Anomalies like this." He grimaces, but I wonder if it's heartfelt. My father enjoys a good mystery too much not to be enjoying this at least to some degree.

My thoughts are swirling. Kal is gone. Annika is here. And then it hits me. "But Dad! If Annika is the one who saw Aunt Rae, and she's stuck here in The Realms, then she can't tell anyone about us. That means you can bring back her planet without having to worry about upsetting the natural order of things, or whatever you said before. And then Kal and his parents will come back!"

Dad grips my shoulder. "Joss, I cannot bring her planet back. It does not exist anymore. You must accept it. Kal will always be alive in your memories."

I cringe at his words. I can't accept it, no matter what he says. I have no experience with losing anyone. Immortality in The Realms can be incredibly, mind-numbingly, chew-your-own-foot-off boring, but on the plus side, no death. Except now, apparently, with a chain of events that started with some girl looking in the wrong spot at the wrong time and ended with my best friend going *poof*, never to be seen again.

I shake my head. "There must be something—"

"She's waking up," Dad says, cutting me off. "Go over there and convince her this is still a dream."

But I don't move. I don't want to talk to the girl ever again. All of this—ALL OF IT—is her fault. I've never ignored a direct order from my father before, but I just can't do it. I dig my heels into the floor. Literally, I push them in a few inches.

Dad scowls. "You don't have a choice, Joss. If she figures out where she is, who knows what the cosmic consequences would be. At the very least she can't know what happened to her planet, her family and friends. It's up to you to protect her. To protect The Realms."

Dad always did have a flair for the dramatic. How am I

supposed to take care of this girl? Mom won't even let us have a pet even though we all promised to help take care of it. Forget a pet, she won't even let me have a plant! I'm about to dig my heels in even further, when a gasp from across the room diverts our attention.

Annika is standing in front of the huge window, staring wide eyed at the billions of galaxies swirling before her. Slowly, she lifts her arm and points straight out at them. "WHAT in the WORLD is THAT?"

Our truest life is when we are in dreams awake.
—Henry David Thoreau, philosopher

5

I know Annika can see the billions of blobs of light hanging in the blackness of space, some very close, some so distant they are hard to make out, even for me. And the blobs, the galaxies, are of course magnificent. But that's not really the true picture of what's out there. The dark parts of space are glowing, too, with the heat from the very birth of the universe. For perhaps the first time in my life I am struck by how lucky we are in The Realms to be able to truly *see*.

She taps her foot.

I try to remember what someone from Earth would call what lies beyond Dad's see-through wall. We'd call it the universe. Everything that exists, as far as we know. Before I can try to explain it, she presses her face right up to the transparent panel. "Are those . . . galaxies? Those swirling things? Like the Milky Way?"

"Yes. Each one has billions of stars."

"And how . . . how many galaxies are there?"

I shrug. "A few hundred billion, I think. More are still forming."

Across the room my father clears his throat and I remember my duty here. I force myself to smile, when really I want to yell and scream and tell her what she's done. "Great job on that, by the way," I say in the breeziest voice I can muster.

"On what?" she asks, not tearing her eyes away from the trillions of glowing stars surrounding us.

"On dreaming up all those galaxies. I see some nebula, too, with some young stars forming. And over there? Nice touch to add that globular cluster."

She blinks, twisting a yellow chain on her wrist back and forth. "*I* made all these?"

I cringe at the very thought of telling her yes, when really it took almost fourteen billion years and an untold number of pies. One low growl from Dad and I say (with much more enthusiasm than I feel), "This is *your* dream. So that means you must have made everything."

When she doesn't answer, I keep going, as much as it pains me. "You made the roof and the floor and that table, too."

Finally tearing herself away from the view, she grins. "I guess I did!" Then she looks me up and down. "So what are you, then, my love interest? Hmm... I'd have thought I would have picked someone, I don't know, *cuter* for my first dream crush."

I frown.

"Don't get me wrong," she says. "Some girls might like you. You're probably not smart enough for my friend Rachel because she's like, a *genius*, but Lydia likes guys with really strange haircuts, so maybe her. Weird that you're in *my* dream, though. Hey! I bet that means Lydia's going to show up!"

While she crawls under the table to search for Lydia, I pout. My hair actually looks a lot better than usual because Aunt Rae tried to straighten it out, and she's very good with scissors. At least I *thought* she was. I peer under the table. "Hey, didn't you say Lydia would hate me for my perfect skin? Which is it? Hate me for my skin or like me for my hair?"

She doesn't reply. She's just sitting, cross-legged, under the center of the table. I sigh and crawl under. "Annika? Are you okay?"

"She's not here," she replies. "Lydia, I mean. If this is my dream, I should be able to make things happen the way I want them to, right?"

"Um, I guess so."

"Maybe I'm stuck in someone *else's* dream."

"Hmm. Well, do you see anyone else you know?"

"I'm under a table! How am I supposed to see anyone I know?"

I shrug. "Then that means it's your dream, I guess."

She squeezes her eyes shut. "Then I want Lydia to appear next to me!"

Lydia, not surprisingly, does not appear.

Annika's shoulders sag.

"Maybe Lydia's in the middle of her own dream," I suggest, "so that's why she can't come." My theory is ridiculous, but she brightens.

"Maybe you're right! I'll try something else."

She eyes me again, tapping her finger on her chin as she thinks. I have a sinking feeling I'm not going to like what comes next.

"Okay," she says. "When I count to three, you will have two noses."

I grimace. Dad is REALLY going to owe me after this. "Two noses?"

She nods. "And the extra one should come out of your chin."

"You want me to have a chin-nose?"

"Yes."

"Fine. But when you wake up from this dream, I hope you feel bad about this choice."

She watches me expectantly. If this is what it takes to convince her she's in a dream, I have no choice. I focus so intently that I get a sharp headache. Instantly I sprout a chin-nose.

She clasps her hands together and squeals in delight.

From under the table I can see Dad walk out the door and close it behind him. I don't blame him. I'm hideous. "Can you get rid of it now?" I ask. "I have to sneeze and that could be really embarrassing."

"It's actually pretty gross to look at," she says. With a wave of her hand she adds, "Be gone, chin-nose! And hello...elbow-eye!"

I make the extra nose disappear but have no intention of adding an eye to my elbow.

"Hmm, that's weird," she says, checking out both my elbows. "It didn't work that time."

I shrug. "Dreams have strange rules. Maybe you only get to change something once a day."

She considers this. "Maybe. But you know what? This is a really long dream. No offense or anything, and you seem like a nice kid, but I'd really, really like to wake up now. I kinda miss my dad, even though he's probably watching me sleep with a disappointed look on his face. I wish he would wake me up. He'd want to hear about how well I can make globular clusters." She tries to smile, but it wobbles and disappears.

For the first time since she arrived I study her face. Kal often got to visit his parents OnWorld, but since I've never left The Realms, I've only seen humans in the Afterlives, where their essence lives on inside a simulated body. But Annika is a living person still, and there are very real differences. For one, if I look closely, I can literally see the deep red blood pulsing in her veins. The Old Ones, like Aunt Rae, would be able to see through her skin and muscles and bones down to the tiniest atom.

I find myself returning to her eyes. They are deep brown,

almost black, and are currently filling with a clear liquid. She wipes at one of them with the back of her hand while trying to make it appear like she's not crying.

This girl is never going to see her father again. She doesn't know this, but I do. Even though Dad and I have a complicated relationship, I can't imagine not seeing him again. Or my mother. I don't even know if Annika has a mother, but if someone told me mine was whooshed out of time forever, I'd do everything in my power to get her back.

My eyes widen. That's exactly how Kal must have felt about *his* parents! Only he never got a chance to get over the shock and start planning. I have to do something! I start to stand, forgetting we're still sitting under the table. I bang my head, which, thanks to the Powers That Be programming our cells to feel things, hurts. A lot.

"Where are you going?" she asks as I rub the spot.

"I have to go find my father."

"You can't just leave me here, in this strange place."

She's right of course.

"Fine. Come with me, then."

She scrambles out from under the table, grabs her jacket, and follows me out the door. We get only two steps down the narrow flagpole-shaped hall when Gluck appears and steers us both by the arm into another doorway. I've never been in this room. It's more closet than room, with only a small table and chair and no windows. On the table sits a tray of food and a planet view screen. It's tuned to an old

Earth television show, something about three yellow-haired girls and three brown-haired boys who have to become a family, or like some kind of *bunch*. A bunch of what? It's a little confusing.

"Hey, my mom has that series on DVD," Annika says, gazing fondly at the screen. "She used to watch it on TV when she was a kid."

I guess she has a mother after all. Had a mother? I feel queasy again.

"Sit," Gluck orders her. "Enjoy. We have a whole bunch of snacks, too."

I can just picture one of Gluck's assistants frantically running around trying to find out what kids from Earth like to eat. He watches anxiously as Annika peeks over the edge of the tray. She points to each plate in turn, her voice rising at each discovery. "A Twinkie. A mug of hot chocolate. Marshmallow squares. A bagel with cream cheese and Red Hots on top. And, for the main course, a turkey club on rye with a pickle! Wow, you guys really know the way to a girl's heart!" She flashes me a smile. "Maybe I *can* stay in this dream a little longer."

Visibly relieved that he got it right, Gluck pulls out the chair for her. She sits and begins to stuff the yellow cake she called a Twinkie into her mouth. It looks equal parts delicious and disturbing. Soon she is happily watching the screen and sipping her drink. Gluck puts his finger to his lips and pulls me back into the hall.

"What's going on?" I ask as Gluck quietly closes the door. "I really need to talk to my dad. I need to get Kal back right away."

"Wait," he says. "I need to talk to you first."

"I can't. And I can't babysit this girl much longer. I feel bad lying to her."

I turn to go but he shoots in front of me. The hallway is so narrow, he fills the whole space. I have no choice but to hear him out.

"I agree with you," he says. "About the importance of getting your friend and his parents back. I'd bet your father does, too, but he can't let on. These rules are as old as time. He can't set a precedent by going against them simply because friends are involved. It would show weakness, and that is something your father would never do. Ever." He glances behind him, then lowers his voice. "But I'll help you because, well, I really like their beaches." He lowers it even further. "And fantasy football."

I give him my full attention now. "But I thought you said it was too late, that the whole solar system is completely gone?"

"Oh, it is. No trace that it ever existed. So what we'll do is this—I'll keep the PTB off your trail for as long as I can. We'll temporarily suspend your pie delivery services so none of the view screens will show your activity. You won't be able to tell anyone what you're doing, of course, not even your brothers."

Laughter comes from the closet-room, and a slurping-through-a-straw noise follows. I lower my voice. "How can I tell them what I'm doing if I have no idea what you're talking about?"

He glances around to make sure we're still alone. "You'll be rebuilding it, of course."

I stare at his face and am reminded of Annika's garbage-disposal comment. But even his bizarre appearance can't distract me from his words. "You want me to rebuild Earth?"

"No."

"That's a relief."

"I want you to rebuild the entire solar system," he says. "And quickly, because the PTB catch on fast to any unusual activities. You'll have to make it exactly the way it was before. But this time, Annika can't be allowed to look in that telescope and find The Realms. It's your only chance. It's *humanity's* only chance."

Okay, Gluck the Yuck is officially insane. "That's totally impossible. How am I supposed to rebuild Earth and its solar system exactly the way it was? Any tiny little change and the whole thing could turn out different. I only got a C in Planet Building class. I couldn't possibly do this."

"But you can," he insists. "All you need to do is figure it out by working backward."

"Backward? Backward from *what*?"

He twitches his thumb toward the closed door. "From her."

I see nothing in space as promising as the view from a Ferris wheel.

—E. B. White, writer and editor

6

If anyone had told me two hours ago that I'd walk into PTB headquarters with Kal and come out with a human girl from Earth, I'd have said they'd eaten too many fulu berries from that one garden in The Realms where the fruit tastes a little funky. But here we are, strolling down the street together like it's not completely unnatural and bizarre. Every few feet Annika stops to point at something else.

"That playground looks just like the one by my school!" she says. Or, "Look! That house is like my grandmother's house in Arizona! Except my grandmother's house is yellow with shutters and a driveway, and that one is green without shutters and no driveway."

All I can do is nod and say, "Really, wow, dreams sure are weird that way." Other than the streets themselves, which are still translucent, The Realms have been redesigned to look like Earth. This happens anytime a planet dies off. We like to pay our respects. Plus it gets really boring looking at the same things for SO many eons, so we jump at any chance to redecorate.

Gone are the shimmering dome-shaped houses and buildings, the multicolored clouds. Gone are the huge sculptures that normally dot our landscape. Judging by the amount of detail I see around us—the vegetables in the gardens, the hand-painted signs on the storefronts—it's clear people have put in extra effort this time. This is good for Annika, since her surroundings feel familiar and she's clearly not as scared as she might otherwise be.

"I think I figured out why I'm stuck in this dream," she says.

I'm too busy glaring behind me at the ever-thickening crowd to ask for her theory. The crowd stares and points at Annika like she has a giant sunflower growing out of her head, which is kind of insulting to the Florapods from the Large Magellanic Cloud Galaxy, who actually DO have flowers growing out of their heads. Word had gone out via the communication network for everyone to pretend it's perfectly normal to have a human in The Realms, so I give the group of gawkers one last glare, and they finally turn away.

Annika is still talking, something about drinking too much of the coffee her dad had made so he could stay awake for the Mars approach and how coffee can have the opposite effect on teenagers. I mumble something akin to "Oh, yeah, maybe, sure" but I'm only half-listening. I need to ask

Gluck more questions. A lot more questions. I must be the absolute *last* guy in The Realms who should be responsible for bringing back a planet. To say nothing of a whole solar system. If Kal's going to have any chance of coming back to life, he's going to need someone who actually has a clue what to do. Any of my six brothers would have a better shot. They get out in the universe a lot more than I do, which is never. I need to convince Gluck he has the wrong person while there's still time.

I make an interested-sounding grunt when Annika points to a tree that reminds her of a tree she used to swing from during the summer she was eight. At this rate I'll have aged another million years before we make it to Kal's house. Gluck told me he sent word to Aunt Rae that Kal had left suddenly on a last-minute trip to visit his parents on their current research trip. If she knew the truth, she would completely break down. She's very sensitive. Maybe that's why she makes such good pies. To keep them both occupied, Gluck arranged for Aunt Rae to watch over Annika until we can figure out what to do with her.

We pass a meadow of grazing horses, a swimming pool, a used-car lot, two town squares, and a shopping mall before reaching Kal's neighborhood. Annika stumbles backward as a walk-in phone booth pops up right in front of us. She stares at it. "I haven't seen one of those since I was a little kid," she muses. "Why would I put that in my dream?"

"Who knows?" I say, anxious to keep her from focusing on anything too closely. I steer her around the phone booth and can't help noticing that Dad was right—her arm is more solid than anything I've ever felt before. It feels strange but interesting, and I almost don't want to let it go. She solves that problem by shaking my hand off and pointing excitedly at a Ferris wheel that has just sprouted up across the street.

I position myself between her and the street. "We should keep moving. It will be dark soon."

It won't. It never gets dark in The Realms.

"Let's ride it," she says. "We'll only go around a few times, okay?" Then she laughs. "What am I asking you for? You're just a figment of my imagination!"

Before I can argue, she grabs me by the hand and yanks me across the street. I've never held a girl's hand before. Especially not a REAL hand, with a pulse beating through it. This day seriously can't get any stranger.

I let her drag me to the entrance of the Ferris wheel because I am too distracted by the weight of her hand to fight it. I guess Gluck can wait a little longer.

We join the long line waiting for the ride. The sudden loss of her hand in mine makes me feel even lighter than usual, almost like I could float away. I grind my feet into the grass to shake off the feeling. As soon as everyone sees us—the seventh son of the Supreme Overlord and the human girl from Earth—they quickly part and usher us to the front of the line.

"*I* did that!" Annika says proudly as we reach the entrance. "I wished for them to move, and they did!"

I'd roll my eyes but that is a gesture better left to about-to-be-teenage girls from Earth. "Uh-huh," I say instead. "You are truly Master of the Dream World."

The ride operator turns out to be none other than my second-oldest (and most popular, charming, handsome, cheerful, blah blah blah) brother, Grayden. He grins as Annika climbs into the small metal carriage. His ridiculously bright green eyes sparkle in that annoying way of his. "Aren't you going to introduce me, little bro?"

I climb in behind Annika. "Aren't you supposed to be off inspiring great artists?"

"I'm on dinner break. They'll have to create their masterpieces without me." He keeps his eyes on Annika, who, I'm not surprised to see, is blushing.

"This is your brother?" she asks, leaning over. "Now, *he* would make a good love interest."

"We don't want to hold up the ride," I snap, securing the safety bar across our laps even though it's completely unnecessary. You can't get too seriously injured in The Realms. If we fell, our atoms would just sink into the ground and then pop back out into our shape. Well, I guess hers wouldn't, seeing as she's so solid. I test the bar to make sure it's tight.

Grayden waves good-bye as the carriage starts to creak upward. Annika leans over the side to wave back. It's fine with me if she'd prefer him. I'm used to the rest of my family getting all the attention, and that's how I like it. I go to school, deliver my pies, and hang out with Kal. That's my day. Every day. Maybe it's not the most exciting of lives, but it works for me. It's comfortable. Now I'm on a Ferris wheel, of all things, with a girl whose heart I can hear beating from a foot away. I can tell by their faces that all the people on the ground can hear it, too. If she has her volumizer on, Aunt Rae could even hear it as she waits for us. It echoes like a drum, pounding out a message. *I'm still here. I'm still here.* The only one of its kind left of her world. I try to tune it out.

"You can see the whole *city* from here!" Annika exclaims as we reach the top. She leans forward to ooh and aah, Grayden and his charms apparently forgotten.

Rather than explaining how insulting it is for her to refer to The Realms as a mere *city*, I let it go and look around us. As far as my eyes can see (and they can see FAR), The Realms are now a hodgepodge of brick buildings and wooden houses, storefronts and evergreen forests, movie theaters and train stations with trains that really wouldn't take you anyplace. My school, usually a free-floating dome, is now a petting zoo complete with kittens, goats, ducks, and a man in a bunny suit selling food pellets.

None of these things exist anymore. Not on Earth, any-way. Everything we're looking at was pulled from records made by OnWorlders like Kal's parents. I squeeze my eyes shut to block it all out.

"Oh, you get motion sickness!" Annika says, sounding concerned. "My little brother, Sam, gets that." She points away from me. "If you need to throw up, please do it in *that* direction."

Before I can protest that I am *not* motion sick, she leans out and yells to Grayden. "Hey down there! Joss is about to toss his cookies! Get me outta this thing!"

I close my eyes and lean back. Oh, how I wish this really WAS a dream. But the giggles I hear below assure me that it's not. This will give Grayden material to tease me with for the next thousand years, at least.

No one can confidently say that he will still be living
tomorrow.
                                    —Euripides, playwright

7

"A re you feeling okay, little bro?" Grayden teases as we climb off the Ferris wheel. "Maybe you should go lie down until your stomach feels better. I can take Annika for some ice cream." He motions with his head to an ice cream stand that has popped up nearby. His hair flops in front of his eyes, and he brushes it aside. I'm more aware than ever of my stupid haircut. The next people in line give one last chuckle at my expense, then climb into our carriage.

Annika considers the offer, twirling her hair around her finger.

"I feel fine," I snap. "No time for ice cream, anyway. We need to get to Kal's house. Annika is going to stay with Aunt Rae."

Grayden looks over my shoulder. "Where is that sidekick of yours, anyway? You and Kal are usually joined at the hip. Is he still working down at the Afterlives after school?"

I swallow hard. "Kal is...he's OnWorld. Visiting his parents. It was a last-minute thing."

Grayden nods. "Lucky stiff."

I'm afraid if I speak again he'll know something's wrong.

Annika looks between us, her brow furrowing. "What are you guys talking about? Afterlives? OnWorld? This dream isn't making much sense."

"Oh, you know how dreams are," Grayden says without missing a beat. "It's a sign of intelligence if you have complicated dreams. Anyone could dream about forgetting to study for a test, or showing up at school naked. But to dream up a whole world where people talk about things that don't make sense? That's like, genius time."

"Really?" she says, smiling broadly. "I mean, I got mostly A's last marking period, and I taught my little brother to add and subtract when he was only three, but I don't know about *genius*. I'm no Albert Einstein."

"We really should go," I tell her, anxious to leave before Grayden offers to take her to the Afterlives to visit the real Einstein. The Afterlives are totally in the other direction.

"What's the rush?" he asks. "I have a few more minutes before my next gig. Ice cream is very refreshing. Tastes even better in a dream, right, Joss?" He elbows me, but I ignore him. A throng of kids have gathered around the ice cream stand, talking excitedly and licking their cones. It really does look refreshing. Just because we don't have to eat very much in The Realms doesn't mean we don't like a good cold treat when we stumble across one.

I shake my head. "Aunt Rae is waiting, and she probably made dinner. We don't want to be rude."

"Okay, okay," he says, holding up his palms in defeat. "I give up. Joss here is right. He's always very considerate, especially to his elders."

It's risky hanging around Grayden too long because you never know what's going to come out of his mouth.

And of course he's not done. "Brave, strong, brilliant, truly a shining example of a boy on the cusp of manhood. Why, just last week, he—"

"That's enough," I say, pulling Annika away before my brother finishes telling whatever embarrassing story he was planning to share.

"He seems nice," Annika says, looking back over her shoulder as I drag her away.

I grunt, not ready to discuss the complicated relationship between a "boy on the cusp of manhood" and his six older brothers.

We cross the street. I glance back to see that Grayden and the entire Ferris wheel are gone. A 3-D holographic image of Earth hovers in its place, blinking in and out of existence. I hurry her around the nearest corner so she doesn't see it. She's going to figure out sooner or later this isn't a dream, that however smart or creative she thinks she is, she couldn't have dreamed up The Realms. I'd rather this realization not happen on my watch, though. I pick up the pace and we round the corner to Kal's house.

Normally, his house is shaped like a pie with windows (Aunt Rae finds the shape peaceful). Now it resembles one of the huge granite heads from Mount Rushmore. I'm glad it looks different than usual. Maybe being here won't remind me of Kal so much now. "Abraham Lincoln!" Annika exclaims. "Cool! And I like the garden gnome."

She points to a small bearded creature made of wood and holding a shovel. Must be an Earth thing. In addition to Aunt Rae's usual colorful garden, her lawn is now covered in simulated Earth grass.

We enter through the president's left nostril, which is a narrow tunnel that deposits us into the living room. I'm disappointed to see that nothing has changed on the inside of the house. Kal's drumsticks still lay askew on the ground, right where he'd tossed them when the sirens wailed. Seeing them feels like a punch in the gut. The drumbeats from the last time he played run through my mind. I can almost still hear them here in the room. Right now I'd happily listen to him bang on the drums for the next five hundred years if only he'd return home.

Aunt Rae comes rushing out of the kitchen to greet us, and the drumbeats fade to nothingness. I want to run and hug her like I used to when I was little. Instead, for her sake, I have to pretend that Kal is just fine OnWorld somewhere. And we *both* have to pretend that Earth is still there and that this is a dream, for Annika's sake. I shake my head to clear it. It's all very confusing.

Aunt Rae's volumizer is noticeably absent. She sees me looking at her ear and says, "I got my hearing fixed. After what happened, well, I couldn't take a chance like that again." She glances at Annika, then turns away as tears fill her eyes.

"Hey, I know this place," Annika says, peeking around Aunt Rae into the kitchen. "This is from my earlier dream. The one with the old lady. Hey, that was you!"

Aunt Rae blinks away her tears and forces a smile. "How lovely. I've never been in anyone's dream before."

This is certainly true.

Annika yawns.

"Come," Aunt Rae says, steering Annika toward Kal's room. "You must be tired from the shock of..."

I clear my throat.

"I mean, from such a long dream," she finishes.

Annika nods. "My mom always warned me that coffee could do weird things to teenagers."

"I thought you were only twelve," I say.

She glares at me. "My thirteenth birthday's in two weeks. I totally count as a teenager."

I'm about to say something mean about how two weeks here won't bring her even the slightest bit closer to thirteen, but Aunt Rae shakes her head at me disapprovingly. I can't help it. I know Annika wasn't aware of the destruction her actions would rain down upon her entire civilization (and on Kal's parents, and then on Kal, and then on me), but I still blame her for what happened. I better leave before I say something I'll regret.

I lag behind as Aunt Rae guides Annika into Kal's old room. I have no need for another reminder of his absence.

"This looks just like my real room," Annika says sleepily.

I find it hard to believe that Kal's room—home to one of the finest comic-book collections in all of The Realms, not to mention some really cool gadgets his parents have brought back from the more advanced civilizations—has any similarities to hers.

I wonder if it would be rude if I were to slip out now. Aunt Rae seems to have everything under control. I'm half-way through the president's nose when Annika calls out, "Joss, I want to give you something."

I groan and trudge back down the hall. Annika is standing in the doorway of the bedroom, which, I can't help but notice, is pink and white with a frilly canopy over the bed.

Kal's bedroom is definitely NOT normally pink and white with a frilly canopy over the bed. I should have figured Aunt Rae would have redecorated for her houseguest.

"What's that?" I ask, pointing to a rectangular object on the wall. It has images tacked to it—flat two-dimensional ones, of a house and a car and a baby and an airplane and many more. It's in the same spot where Kal had taped up a holograph of one of his favorite bands. He had to trade a lot of cool equipment for that, so I hope wherever the poster is, it's safe.

"If you must know," Annika says, barely glancing at the wall, "it's my vision board."

"Vision board?"

"You haven't heard of a vision board?" Without waiting for my reply, she goes on. "It's a map for my life. You know, how I want things to go. I graduate with honors, go to college, get an awesome job, get married, have a kid or two, see the world."

I stare at it, mesmerized. Plans for the future. I've never made any of those. The future just isn't a thing here. It's always so far away that there's no reason to even think about it.

"Here," Annika says, holding out a short, yellow chain. I recognize it as the one she had been nervously twisting earlier.

I force my eyes from the vision board and take the chain. Made of tiny links, it feels cold to my fingers, and hard. "What is it?" I ask, bouncing it in my palm.

"It's my grandmother's favorite bracelet. When she died last year, my father gave it to me."

"Why are you giving me your grandmother's favorite bracelet?"

She shrugs. "I feel bad about before. You know, about flirting with Grayden. My friend Jessica has a superhot brother, and it drives her crazy when her friends flirt with him."

"That was flirting?"

She reaches out and snatches the bracelet from my palm. "I'll take it back, then. It's real gold, ya know."

Actually, I didn't know, having never seen real gold before. The Realms were formed long before stars started exploding and showering space with the heavier elements. We have samples of everything, of course, but not jewelry, as far as I know. I had liked the way it felt. So solid and smooth. "No, I'll keep it," I say, grabbing it back.

Or at least I *try* to grab it back. Sometime between my reaching and her pulling away, the bracelet disappears. I look questioningly at Aunt Rae, who shakes her head. If she didn't do it, then where did it go?

Annika grins. "I'm getting better at controlling this dream thing!"

Aunt Rae and I share a doubtful look, but we don't contradict her.

Annika holds up her wrist, then slowly lowers it. "Hmm, I figured it would have gone back on there." Puzzled, she crawls around on the white carpet (Kal's was black), then stands and shrugs. "I'm going to take a nap. I fully expect to wake up back home this time, with my bracelet back on my wrist. Adios, dream folk!"

"No dinner?" Aunt Rae asks her, clearly disappointed. She finally has a chance to feed someone who actually needs to eat to survive.

"No, thanks," Annika says. "I filled up on junk food earlier." She grabs a bathrobe from the foot of the bed and slips it on over her clothes. "Nice!" she says to herself as she ties the sash around her waist. "I thought I lost this belt." She climbs into bed, turns her back to us, and instantly falls asleep.

Aunt Rae and I watch the lump in the bed slowly rise and fall, then tiptoe out of the room. "How is she breathing?" she whispers as we head down the hall.

"I wondered the same thing."

"Strange times we live in," she says. "So, can I interest you in an open-faced hot turkey sandwich, gravy, stuffing, and cranberry sauce?"

I shake my head. I really have to get back to Gluck. As she walks me to the nostril, I ask, "Why do you think that bracelet disappeared? Is it because it was made out of gold? Like it wasn't compatible with The Realms or something?"

Aunt Rae shakes her head. "If only that were the case."

"Why, then?"

She hesitates before answering. "It's because Annika's grandmother is also gone now. I felt her go. So anything that belonged to the dear old woman would disappear as if it never existed. Which I suppose it didn't." She sighs. "I find the rules of time exceedingly confusing."

Messing with the time stream is almost never done for that reason. "What do you mean, her grandmother's gone? Annika said she died last year, right? So she'd be in the Afterlives, or at least her essence would. Or part of it. I don't really know how that all works."

Aunt Rae shakes her head sadly but says no more.

*If you've never eaten while crying you don't know
what life tastes like.*

—Johann Wolfgang von Goethe, writer

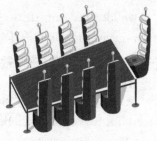

8

I should be knocking on Gluck's door right now, demanding that he explain why Annika's grandmother is gone from the Afterlives, and convincing him I am not the man to fix all this. Instead, I am at my own front door because Mom has only one rule: Do not miss family dinner, no matter what. Oh, and I have to clock in whenever I come or go, because she insists it's the only way she can keep track of so many boys. Even my father has to do it.

I stand in front of the face reader, and an image of my face is projected on all the view screens around the house. A cheer rises from the kitchen. It's been like this every day of my life. It started because my mom felt guilty that all the brothers had someone they could boss around except for me. When I was younger, I loved all the attention that came with being the youngest. Now that I'm a teenager I could happily do without it. A glance at the wall shows me that everyone has clocked in except for Dad.

I hurry down the long corridor to the kitchen, passing the hundreds of childhood holographs that Mom displays on the walls. I avert my eyes when a picture of me in a particularly awkward growth period pops up. I plan to eat quickly and hurry back out. How am I supposed to be around my mother and not tell her about Kal? She always knows if something's wrong. All I can do is try to act normal.

All my brothers are seated in their usual spots: Thade across from our father's currently empty seat, then Grayden, Ty, Laz, Ash, and Bren. As the youngest, I slip into my seat at the end. Usually I'd start talking to Bren, who is the one brother I confide in. But now there's so much I have to hold back. I give him a quick smile instead.

"You look different," Bren says, studying me. Then he calls across the table. "Hey, Ty! Does Joss look different to you?"

Ty looks up from his plate. "He does have a certain glow to him."

"That's what getting his first girlfriend will do to a guy," Grayden says before swallowing a big swig of liquid spice.

The others laugh. I should have known Grayden would tell everyone about seeing me with Annika. "She's not my girlfriend!" I insist.

"Boys!" my mother snaps. "How many times have I told you not to tease your brother?"

They laugh again. We all know it's a very high number.

"Four billion and three," Thade replies. No one argues.

Thade, the oldest, is never wrong. His calculations are always perfect. That's why it's his job to make sure all the planets stay in orbit around their suns.

"Exactly," Mom says. "You think you'd learn by now." She piles heaping spoonfuls of a brownish stew onto my plate. Mom has many talents, but cooking isn't one of them. Since we could eat once a month and get all the energy and nutrition we need, dinner is all about "family time," or so she claims.

She takes her seat across from us at the table and beams at me. "So, Joss...when do I get to meet your new girlfriend?"

"Mom!"

The brothers laugh again.

She shrugs. "Sorry. It's a mother's job to care."

I dig into my stew, despite the fact that it tastes like the sole of my shoe.

"Where's Dad?" Thade asks.

I pause from chewing, surprised at the question. Thade isn't yet a member of the PTB, but he always knows everything that goes on. Is it possible he doesn't know that three immortals have been lost today? I'm not certain if I'm supposed to keep that a secret or not. I glance at Mom to see her response to Thade's question. If she doesn't say anything, then I won't. Her eyes well up, but she quickly plants a smile on her face. It's a familiar smile. It means "*I really know more than what I'm about to say.*"

"I'm sure it's been a big day down at headquarters," she

finally says. "What with losing more than eight million different species from a single planet."

We all stop eating at that. "Eight *million*?" I ask. I know there are millions of species in the universe, but I didn't know one planet could have that many.

She nods. "And the inhabitants of Earth hadn't even discovered most of them yet. Now they will never get the chance." She squares her shoulders. "But I'm sure it couldn't be helped. Rules are rules. The girl broke the fundamental laws of physics."

Laz snorts. "Last I checked, the fundamental laws of physics don't say anything about pulling planets out of time because they don't want to deal with what might happen if people knew about us."

Our mother throws him a hard look and he returns to his food. As the fourth son, Laz is in a difficult position. He's not grouped with the three older boys, or the three younger, and his job (creating sunrises and sunsets) is a solitary one. He kind of gets forgotten about. I think that's why he has these little outbursts sometimes. He likes to remind everyone that he's here. Still, even Laz wouldn't criticize Dad's decisions to his face. Not even when Dad decided that everyone in The Realms should communicate only through hand gestures for nearly two hundred years. The novelty of that wore off very quickly, but we had to stick it out. Dad is stubborn and he never reverses an order.

The sounds of drumbeats begin to echo in my head again, like they had at Aunt Rae's. I glance around to see if anyone else hears it, but no one shows any signs of it. I shake my head to clear it.

The awkward silence around the table is broken by Mom reminding me to drink more water. I gulp down my glass and stand up to leave.

Mom points to my chair. I sigh and sit back down. "Being assigned to watch after the human girl is a big honor," she says. "I hope you let the PTB know how grateful you are for this opportunity."

I think back. Nope, gratitude was not on my list of emotions.

"At least tell us what she's like," Mom says.

I throw up my hands. "I don't know. She's like any girl, I guess. Kind of weird. Talks a lot."

"Is she pretty?" Bren asks.

Next to Grayden, Bren is the most girl-crazy. He's also my favorite brother and the one who's the nicest to me. Although right now I wish he would focus on something else. "How am I supposed to know? I really don't want to talk about it."

"She's pretty," Grayden confirms. "In a human sort of way."

Bren chews thoughtfully then nods. "Head slightly too small for her body?"

"Exactly."

"Freaky," Bren says.

"Totally," Ty and Laz agree. Thade refrains from replying because he is above this sort of thing, and Ash is too busy reading from the book hidden in his lap. He is the quietest of all of us, and the most studious. He's the go-to guy for homework.

I stand up. "This is why I didn't want to talk about it. Mom, can I go now?"

"Yes, go. Have fun with Kal, but don't be home too late. Tomorrow is Family Picture Day."

A groan rises from the table at the mention of the holographer coming over for yet another round of terrible pictures. I'd complain, too, if it weren't for her mention of Kal. I stop in my tracks and look closely at her. Is she saying that to cover for me so the brothers wouldn't find out? She may not be the warm, fuzzy, hug-you-till-it-hurts type of mother, but at some point during dinner she surely would have tried to comfort me. I was so busy dodging questions about Annika that the thought hadn't occurred to me until now. There's only one other option.

She knows what happened to Earth, but she doesn't know about Kal or his parents. Dad didn't tell her! I give a quick nod and run from the kitchen. Dad has a lot of explaining to do.

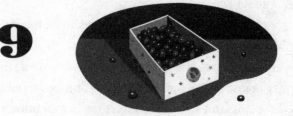

9

ad's office door is firmly closed, and he won't answer my knocks.

"It's really important," I insist to his secretary, Faye.

She continues to ignore me. Faye always ignores me. Truly, I could be on fire and she would continue to file her nails with her heels up on the desk.

I try again. "Life or death kind of important."

"Sorry," she finally says in that clipped voice of hers. "Your father gave strict orders that no one is to disturb him. He's very busy."

I stare her down. "I can hear him hitting golf balls out the window."

She shrugs. "Maybe he is, maybe he isn't."

I glance back at Dad's closed door, tempted to open it without her permission. She sees me looking and gives me a slight shake of the head. "Fine," I say, defeated. "I'm going to see Gluck, then."

"Suit yourself," she says, waving me off down the hall. The *thwack* of the golf club hitting the ball out into space follows me. Dad's usual stress buster is to visit the Afterlives and race with the winged Pelinata from Borga 3. The golf is in honor of Earth, no doubt. I wish he'd be less interested in honoring it and more interested in saving it.

I find Gluck sitting behind his desk stuffing the last piece of what looks like one of Annika's marshmallow squares into his mouth. He sees me and quickly swallows.

"Made extra," he explains, licking the sticky marshmallow off his fingers. "Want one?" He holds out the plate. "They're quite delicious."

I shake my head. "No, thank you. I really need to talk." I begin to pace back and forth. Gluck's office is not nearly as big as Dad's, but there's a nice view of the courtyard. Usually filled with samples of exotic flowers and plants from around the universe, it has been transformed into a minor-league baseball field. Inhabitants of The Realms can play every sport, but the ones with balls are our favorites. Every few seconds a cheer rises from the crowd. I am envious. They get to enjoy this human pastime, while I'm stuck up here with life and death at stake. Mostly death.

Gluck motions for me to close the door, then says, "I know you're probably very upset over Kal."

"Probably?"

"Okay, you're definitely upset. And rightly so. Are you ready to get to work to get him back?"

I try to stand as straight as possible (Mom says I slouch like an old lady) and look him in the eye. "You have to find someone else, Gluck. I deliver pies. That's my job. I'm not the right person for this."

"Who is, then?"

"The PTB. My father. You! Anyone but me!"

He shakes his head. "As far as the PTB and your father are concerned, the case is officially closed. It's back to work as usual. The consequences for viewing The Realms were dealt out, in a very sensible manner, I may add. Still, I was willing to nudge you in the right direction, but I'm afraid that's all I can do. You must trust this decision was the best one. The only one."

I can't believe everyone can just move on so easily! "Okay, let's put Kal aside for a second," I say, beginning to pace again. "What about his parents? They've supplied the PTB with information for millennia. Going from world to world. Filing reports. Collecting samples. Half of what we know about the inhabited planets came from them. Now the PTB's just going to forget about them?"

"Of course not," Gluck says, shuffling through some papers on his desk. He finds what looks like a blueprint and holds it up. "We're planning this lovely statue outside in the park."

I stare at the rudimentary drawings of Kal's parents.

They are wearing short ceremonial robes, like the kind the PTB wear to important meetings. Kal's mother won't even wear shorts when it gets hot OnWorld. She says her legs are too pale to be seen by anyone with eyes. Only an OnWorlder would think something like that. Still, I know she would never want to be memorialized this way. "A statue? That's all they get? A *statue*?"

He crumbles up the plan and tosses it over his shoulder into the trash. "You're right. It's not enough. Look, Joss. If you want to fix this, you need to start soon. You have a big job ahead of you."

I grip the back of the chair. "But I can't possibly do what you're asking. C in Planet Building class, remember? Sixth smartest out of seven brothers? That's the same as second dumbest, you know."

He shakes his head. "You're not dumb, you've just never had to try. There's a difference." He leans forward. He could use a breath mint. "Look. Your brothers would have an easier go of this, I agree. But we can't risk taking them away from their current jobs. That leaves you. Only the sons of the Overlord could possibly have enough power to achieve something on this scale. Plus, you're the one who cares the most. No one else has lost their best friend."

I rub my head. It's still sore from when I tried to stand up under the table, and now Gluck is making it hurt more. I get the sense there are things he's not saying. Doesn't he know I don't have any power? That's why I'm stuck delivering pies!

"What about Annika?" I ask. "She lost everyone, even if she doesn't know it yet. And now her grandmother disappeared from the Afterlives. Did you know that?"

He nods grimly. "They're all going, slowly. All the humans. The more recent arrivals will go first, but one by one, they will all disappear as though they never existed. Which, of course, they didn't. I mean..." He trails off, rubbing his head. "The laws of time. Very confusing."

"But that's so unfair!"

He nods. "An unfortunate consequence of events, I agree."

We stare miserably at each other. He may have a face like a garbage disposal, but at least he has the decency to be upset at the situation. My father's in there practicing his golf swing.

"How is Annika doing?" Gluck asks.

I shrug. "She's with Aunt Rae. Seems okay, I guess. I don't know how much longer she's going to believe this whole dream thing."

"Is she exhibiting any strange behavior?"

"Define *strange*."

"I'm not certain. Passing out, gasping for breath."

I shake my head. "She falls asleep really easily, though."

He nods. "Yes, that would make sense."

None of it makes sense. "Speaking of Annika, how can she breathe here? How can she even walk? We have barely any gravity. Certainly not enough to keep someone as solid as her on the ground."

He hesitates, then says, "Annika's probably not going to be here much longer."

"You're sending her home?" I ask, then realize she has no home to go to. "You mean she's going to disappear, too? Like the humans in the Afterlives?"

He shakes his head. "I just meant, she isn't going to ... you know, *be here much longer.*"

I cross my arms. "Sixth smartest, remember? You're going to have to spell it out for me."

He sighs. "Fine. I worked it out after you left. The only reason she's still alive is because her brain believes she's dreaming. Like most things here in The Realms—and everything on the quantum level—Annika exists right now in a state of possibility. Once that illusion is gone, her body will realize it does not have the nutrients here that it needs. She will panic. Her heart will beat faster in an attempt to use all the remaining oxygen in her system. Her sight will go next. Then she will lose consciousness. Soon after, she will die. Is that clear enough?"

I stare at him. Will he ever tell me *good* news? "There's got to be something we can do to save her."

"This is not your problem, Joss. You have enough to take on."

Then why does it feel like my problem? "I can't just let her die."

"Well, there's not much you can do other than keep the illusion going. Over time we could probably construct a temporary artificial environment from materials

OnWorlders bring from planets similar to hers, but then she'll be confined to a very small space, like a goldfish in a bowl. She'll be fine as long as she never knows where she really is."

"I don't know how much longer that's going to work."

"Then the faster you rebuild her planet, the better chance you have of keeping her alive."

So much for it not being my problem. "What did you mean earlier when you said I should work backward from her?"

He holds out the plate of marshmallow squares. "Sure you don't want one?"

When I don't reply, he lays it back on the desk. "If you knew the chemical composition of her body, you could figure out what humans are made of. You'll need to know that in order to restart the human race."

He says that so casually, like it's as easy as flipping a switch. "Aren't there records of that kind of stuff?"

He pulls up a holoscreen. Pictures flash in quick succession, then stop on a scene of a picnic, a reddish sun hanging overhead. "If you want to know what makes up a Senturon from Agamos, we can tell you that." The Senturon looks almost humanoid, except for the fact that every inch of it is covered in black scales to absorb the heat from its low-energy star. The pictures move again before settling on another. "Or a Philanops from Glycorus 3." I lean forward. The Philanops has no eyes. "Foggy planet," Gluck explains. "Sonar instead of vision. We could tell you about all these and millions more. But the records on humans were down on Earth with Kal's parents—"

"Why?"

Gluck shrugs. "They said they were working on a special project and needed the data. We do have many, many autosaved recordings showing the evolution of the planet, though. All you have to do is re-create everything, on a much smaller scale, of course. Replace the solar system with the one you make, but be sure Annika doesn't look in the telescope this time. Easy as pie! All problems solved!"

I narrow my eyes. "Pie isn't easy. You know what goes into those things."

"It's an expression."

"And you're sure this will get Kal and his parents back?"

"*Sure* is such a strong word. More like...highly confident." He pauses. "Confidently hopeful?"

My heart sinks. "Even if I could do this, which I can't, I definitely can't do it alone."

He frowns. "If you must ask others for help, make sure they sign a confidentiality agreement."

"What's that?"

"Something that says they won't tell anyone what you're trying to do."

"And what if someone does tell?"

He shrugs. "You get to decide their punishment."

"What if they won't sign it?"

"You're the seventh son of the Supreme Overlord of the Universe. They'll sign it."

He may be overestimating my importance.

"Here are those records." He reaches under his desk and places a large brown box on it. I have to stand on tiptoes to see over the rim. Thousands of holofilms on black data dots no larger than buttons fill the box. I could probably fit fifty just in the palm of my hand. The dates inscribed on them go back 4.6 billion years. I've seen dots like this many times. These records from OnWorlders form the basis of our educational system. Now I need to watch them *outside* of school? This keeps getting better and better.

Gluck stands up and places the box in my hands. Our talk is apparently over.

"I might as well tell you," he says, ushering me toward the door. "We've lost the most recent dot, the one that showed the last few weeks of life on Earth. Looked everywhere for it. Launching an internal investigation, I assure you. Don't know how you'll manage to change the course of events at the end point without it, but I'm sure you'll find a way."

Clutching my box in the hall, I turn around to ask the first of the hundred more questions in my head.

"Good luck, Joss," Gluck says, reaching over the box to pat me awkwardly on the head. "My door's always open."

And with that, he shuts the door in my face.

No one ever told me that grief felt so like fear.
                    —C. S. Lewis, professor and writer

10

Hugging Gluck's huge box of holofilms tight to my chest, I head back to Aunt Rae's. Even though I can barely see over the top of it, I am guided by the *thump thump* of Annika's heartbeat, the smell of freshly baked apple pie, and the desire to steer clear of my brothers. I suppose I could make myself taller for a better view, but I never think of things like that until it's too late. That's another point I should have made to Gluck—I am not a creative problem solver.

Most of the houses I pass have returned to their usual dome shapes, but not Aunt Rae's. After five attempts to squeeze through Lincoln's nostril, I lay the box down in defeat, right next to the garden gnome. The doorway is simply too narrow to fit both me and the box at the same time. I'm about to start pushing it with my foot when I hear a single terrifying shriek, followed by silence. I leap over the box and burst into the house. Aunt Rae and I very nearly collide as she runs toward me.

"What's going on?" I turn in all directions, but I don't see anything unusual. "Did Annika make that noise?"

Aunt Rae nods. "She came out from her nap, had some pie—she loved the cherry—then said she was going back to sleep. Could she be having a nightmare? I've heard of those."

We rush down the hall toward Annika's still-shut door. I reach for the knob, but Aunt Rae clears her throat and points toward a handmade sign tacked on the door: THIS IS NOT THE DOOR YOU'RE LOOKING FOR. KEEP MOVING. I MEAN IT. DON'T EVEN *THINK* OF KNOCKING. "It came with the room," Aunt Rae explains.

I press my ear against the door. I can hear her heart thumping faster than before. Who could blame her for having nightmares after everything she's been through? Better let her sleep, though. I'm about to step away, when Aunt Rae gasps and grabs my arm. "We have to go in there before she . . . before . . . oh, it's too late."

"Why? What's wrong?"

She shakes her head and sags against the wall. A second shriek comes from the room. Ignoring the sign, I fling the door open.

The first thing I see is the empty bed. So much for nightmares. The desk chair is empty, too, as is the floor. Then I spot her sitting in Kal's closet, which is now filled with shapeless flowery dresses dangling from multicolored hangers. Hugging her knees, she rocks back and forth, back and forth. Her pink skin seems to have lost its color completely.

I hurry over. "Annika? What's wrong?"

Still rocking, she points one shaky finger at a holoplayer propped up on the floor in front of her. The screen shows a little curly-haired boy, younger than I ever remember being, fast asleep in his bed. As I watch, the scene changes. He's a toddler now, walking unsteadily toward a beaming man with outstretched hands. Now he's a baby trying to hold on to his bottle. Then a newborn, swaddled in blue cloth. The screen darkens, and a young woman appears, as tall and lanky as Annika. She's leaning against a tree, laughing and holding her round belly.

"Joss, I'm so sorry!" Aunt Rae whispers, pulling me aside. "I should have hidden it better." She wrings her hands, more upset than I've ever seen her. Including the time Kal was turned into the cow pie. Then I realize what she's saying. This room isn't just *similar* to Annika's room at home. It *is* Annika's room, down to the last detail. "The data dot! The one Gluck said was missing! *You* took it so you could replicate her room?"

She nods, her eyes cast downward. "I didn't see the harm. I thought it would help her to believe she was still at home."

"It's okay," I tell her, relieved that the film isn't lost.

Annika has now begun to wail. She clutches at the nearest dress and wipes her eyes on the hem. Her wails turn to gasps. She's clutching her throat. Gluck's words fly back to me. She can't breathe! I sink to my knees next to her.

Gasping for air, she says, "I'm . . . I'm not . . . dreaming . . . am I?"

I start to shake my head but the gasping gets worse. Her eyes grow duller as I watch, the life fading with each beat of her slowing heart. "Yes, you are!" I shout, grabbing her shoulders. "You're totally dreaming!"

She regards me dully. "I..." *Gasp. Cough.* "I'm...not... stupid." *Gasp.*

"Of course you're not. You're just a really good dreamer."

Her eyes roll back in her head until only the whites are visible. She struggles to speak. "I'm...I'm not *this* good."

"Move out of the way!" Aunt Rae yells from behind me. I turn around in time to see her run into the room, a big bucket swinging from her hand. Before Annika's heart can make another slow *thump*, a plume of water arches through the air and hits her square in the face.

Annika raises her arms to protect herself, but it's too late. She's completely drenched. Aunt Rae bends down to grasp Annika's wet head between her hands.

"Can you breathe, dear? Do you feel better at all?"

Annika sputters and spits, but her cheeks are getting pink again. "I think so," she finally says. "But that's really, really hot."

"Sorry about that. I forgot about how sensitive your skin is. It worked only because Joss here supplied the extra gravity needed to break down the water molecules and free the oxygen."

"Huh?" Annika mutters, looking up at me. I shrug. I have no idea what Aunt Rae is talking about. She's getting up there in age, after all.

Aunt Rae strokes Annika's wet hair. "There's enough oxygen floating around you now to allow you to breathe temporarily. A little goes a long way here in The Realms."

Now that she's no longer on her last breath, Annika narrows her eyes at me. "That was my brother, Sam. On that video thingy."

Aunt Rae and I exchange glances, but neither of us replies.

"And he was getting younger and younger, and then he went away."

Unable to meet her eyes, I examine the carpet instead. Why would she choose white carpet? It shows every mark.

"Where did Sam go?" Annika asks, only it's more like a demand. "Tell me where he is. *Please*. The truth."

I glance at Aunt Rae but she's looking off into the distance, rhythmically smoothing her apron. Now I understand how hard it was for my father to tell me what happened to Kal. No one wants to give someone news like this. But how can I keep lying to her? She obviously knows she's not dreaming anymore. Seeing her family on that film, it's like they've been frozen in a sort of ageless eternity, their whole lives compressed into their final breath of existence. "Your brother...everyone's...Earth is..." I trail off and stand up. "I can't do it. I'm sorry."

"I'll explain it to her," Aunt Rae says softly. "Why don't you go and rest on the couch. You've had a long day."

I don't argue. I hurry from the room, not even looking back at Annika. I can't tell her everyone she loves is gone. I hurl myself onto the couch, burying my face in it. I just want to lie here for the next few hundred years when all this will have blown over. The images of Annika's brother won't leave my mind. He looked so peaceful, sleeping in his cozy bed, his arms wrapped around a stuffed purple dinosaur. I try to think of other things. Like the fact that my report for school on my job is due tomorrow. If I'm totally honest with myself (which I rarely am) I'm pretty sure the PTB assigned me to deliver pies because that's all I'm capable of. After all, the hardest part of the job is having the willpower not to eat the pies before I deliver them.

I try to shake the feeling that something about that holofilm doesn't make sense, but I can't figure out what it is. I'm glad I'm not in the room while Aunt Rae explains everything to Annika. I know how I felt losing Kal and his parents, but she lost *everyone*. She's going to be totally devastated. I push my face deeper into the couch. I feel more tired and drained than I ever remember. Thinking about other people's feelings is exhausting. And I slept last month so I know it's not a normal kind of tired.

Thump, bang, thump, rat-a-tat-tat, tzing! I don't know how long the drumbeat has been thumping in the background (again, bad at telling the passage of time), but it must have been a while because my head is starting to hurt in that way it does when Kal plays his "masterpiece" for too long in my presence. *Thump, bang, thump, rat-a-tat-tat, tzing!* It's the same few beats I heard earlier but ignored.

I lift my head from the couch and look around. Maybe

Kal left a recording device somewhere and it started playing? The music doesn't seem to be coming from one direction, though. Each time I turn my head it follows me. Am I going crazy? That wouldn't surprise me.

Thump, bang, thump, rat-a-tat-tat, tzing! I don't know why I ever thought hearing his drumming again would bring me comfort. It only makes me feel worse. It's league night at Thunder Lanes. Kal and I are supposed to be making some kids at school wish they'd never picked up a bowling ball. Instead, I'm hearing phantom drumming in my head. How is that fair?

I put my hands over my ears and shout into the air. "Make it stop! I'll take back any mean thing I ever said about Kal's drum skills. Just make it stop!"

It stops. I slowly pull my hands away from my ears. Silence. Blissful silence in my head. Until...

"Took you long enough!" a voice shouts in my ear.

I'd recognize that voice anywhere.

A universe could form inside this room and we would never know. —Sean M. Carroll, physicist

11

I jump up so fast I have no memory of leaving the couch. "Kal? Kal?" I run around the room, frantic. "Are you here? Are you hiding somewhere?"

"I'm right here!" he shouts.

But he's not. I don't see him anywhere. His voice sounds like it's coming through a long tunnel, all tinny and wobbly. I stop dashing around and just turn in circles. "Kal? Are you invisible?"

"No, I'm in a different place."

"What's going on? Is this really you? Is someone playing a trick on me?" I'd guess one of my brothers, but none of them even knows Kal's missing.

"As if anyone else could play the drums that well!" Kal scoffs, his voice sounding a little clearer now, a bit closer. "It's me, I promise. I'll prove it. Remember that love letter you wrote the girl down the block when we were eight? *Dear Taryn, I know I don't know you that well, but your eyes shine like the third moon of Signus Prime.*"

I stop spinning. "Kal! It's really you!"

"Yes! Finally! Now listen, I don't have long. You wouldn't believe what I had to do to communicate with you and—"

"But why can't I see you? My father said there was no trace of your parents and then you winked out and Gluck said you were gone for good, too." I glance at Kal/Annika's bedroom door, but it's still firmly closed. As tired as I was before, I'm now more awake than I've ever been. "Kal, are you still...alive?" Even with my poor judgment of time, it seems like forever until he answers. And when he does, I can barely hear him.

"I'm in...oth...not...Joss?"

"Kal? I can't hear you! Where *are* you?"

"I'm in...wouldn't believe...rock-and-roll universe... Joss, you have...listen to me."

"What? You're in a place called the rock-and-roll universe? That sounds made up."

"It *is* made up!" he says, suddenly sounding much clearer. "I made it up. I don't know what this place is called. But it's rocking and rolling, and not in a good way. Listen, just let me talk before we lose each other again."

I stay silent, afraid to mess up the connection.

He continues. "I'm in this place—this other universe— and my parents are here, too! There are universes *inside* other universes, Joss! And next to, and behind. There are universes everywhere! You know how we used to think we could reach them if we could hitch a ride with enough gravitons, and then you and Bren got caught trying? Well, it's true! Sort of! It's hard to explain. But it's real!"

"I knew it!" I cry, jumping from one foot to the next. "I knew there had to be other universes! What are they like? Does it look like ours? Do they have The Realms there, too? Wait till I tell Bren!"

"You can't tell anyone!" Kal says sternly. "I don't think we're supposed to be here. I guess since we're immortal, we had to go *somewhere* when Earth disappeared, and somehow we wound up here."

"Are all the people from Earth with you, too?"

"No, it's only us. Listen, my parents said...and... wasn't what..."

"Kal!" I start to turn in circles again. "You're getting all garbled again."

"Don't...other...have to go. Collapsing...slow...think."

"What? What's collapsing? Wait! I'm going to get you back! I have a box of data dots!" I'm aware I'm not making much sense, but I can feel him slipping away so I'm not thinking clearly. "Don't worry, Kal! I'm going to save you!" I strain my ears to listen hard, but I think he's gone.

I keep turning in circles, like that will bring him back. Finally I hear his faint voice say, "Joss! Will keep trying... listen for...drums...wait...don't!" And then nothing. I'm happy and scared and freaked out all at once. He's trapped somewhere, but HE'S NOT DEAD. I don't think I've ever felt this relieved. Well, maybe after the cow pie incident ended. It wasn't very fun being the kid whose best friend was a pile of poop.

"Hey, ballerina boy!" Annika says, snapping her fingers in front of my face.

I stop twirling, dizzy now.

"Come on." She yanks me by my sleeve toward Lincoln's nostril. She leaves a trail of water on the floor behind her. She's wearing one of the shapeless flowery dresses from her closet with the same black clunky boots. It works for her. I'm so relieved about Kal that I could dance. Instead I force myself to act semi-normal because one of us has to. "Where are we going?"

"You're taking me to the Afterlives. Let's get a move on."

Gone is the weepy girl from the closet floor. In her place is the one who stomped angrily on an innocent red parka and told my dad to step off.

Somewhere in between those two extremes would be nice. I pull my arm away as gently as possible. "Your grandmother's not in the Afterlives anymore. Didn't Aunt Rae explain all that?" Maybe she's in shock, that's why she's not screaming and crying. I've heard of this sort of thing before.

She nods impatiently. "We're going to see my grandfather."

"We can't just walk into the Afterlives," I explain. "They don't like visitors. We have to find someone to let us in." Kal used to sneak me in sometimes, but obviously that's not going to work this time.

"So?" she asks, tapping her foot. "Find someone."

I know only one other person who works there. My brother Ty. He is the head of the Wardrobe and Scenery Department. I don't relish the idea of asking him for a favor, but once I start going through the holofilms I'm going to be asking a lot of people for a lot of favors, so I might as well start now. "Fine, let's go."

"Wait," Aunt Rae says, stopping us at the door. "Here, you'll need this." She hands me a bucket of water.

"When Annika starts to dry off, you'll have to dump this on her. This one will last longer. It's supersaturated."

"Really?" I ask, unable to keep the grin from spreading on my face. "I can just dump this on her head?"

"Don't look so excited," Annika says, tugging me through the nostril.

"I'll work on another solution while you're gone," Aunt Rae calls after us.

"No rush," I call back. First Kal's not dead, then I'm granted permission to dump a bucket of water on someone's head without getting in trouble. Things are finally looking up!

"Oomph," Annika grunts, tripping right over the garden gnome, still parked in front of the nose. I put down the bucket and catch her before she hits the ground. We have very fast reflexes in The Realms.

She's slippery, but I hold on and quickly help her regain her balance. "Sorry," I say. "I should have moved that." I'd forgotten how good the solidity of her arms feels. She shakes her arm free of my grip, plops right down on the grass next to Lincoln's beard, and glares up at me.

I kneel beside her. "I said I was sorry. You don't have to look at me like I just stole your new puppy."

"It's not the gnome. I'm mad that you didn't tell me the truth. You let me go on thinking all this came from my imagination." She waves her hands wildly at the dome houses, the colorful sky. "I mean seriously, clouds in every color of the rainbow? I'm supposed to make something like that up?"

"I didn't want to keep lying," I say, hoping she hears the sincerity in my voice. "I really didn't. Ask Gluck."

"Who's *Gluck*?"

"The guy whose face looks like the inside of a garbage disposal?"

She wrinkles her nose. "Oh, that guy."

I shrug. "He's not so bad, actually. He's the only one trying to help me make things right."

"What do you mean, make things right?"

"I'm going to bring back Earth," I tell her, sounding way more confident than I actually feel. "And the sun. And your whole solar system."

"*We're* going to bring it back," she corrects me. "I'm the one who lost everything and everyone I ever cared about. I'm not leaving that job to some strange boy whose head is slightly too big for his body."

My hands fly up to the sides of my head. "My head's not too big for my body!"

She shrugs.

"*Yours* is too small!"

"That's the best comeback you have?" she asks. "That my head is too small?"

We glare at each other. My good mood is souring. I stand up. "Let's go. I want to get this done as quickly as you do."

She doesn't move. This girl is trying my patience.

"Why do you care about making anything right, anyway?" she snaps. "You could just go on your merry way and forget about my tiny little planet."

"No, I can't."

"Why?"

I glance back at the house. Now that Aunt Rae's hearing's fixed, I have to watch what I say around her. "I'll tell you while we walk." I turn to pick up the box of data dots that I'd left by the door. Only it's not there!

I run, frantic, from one side of Lincoln's face to the other. "It's not here!"

"What's not here?" Annika asks, jumping to her feet. "What's wrong?"

"The box of films. All my data dots! It was right here, next to the gnome!"

"What are data dots?"

"Holographic films of the history of your planet. They were our one chance at making this work. I had them, and now they're gone."

"What do they look like?"

I lift up the gnome, as though the box could be hidden there. "Like the buttons on your dress."

"Like this?" she asks, reaching down and plucking a single data dot from the Earth-like grass that still covers Aunt Rae's lawn.

I grab for it. "Yes!"

We both drop to our knees, but after covering the whole lawn, we only find one more dot. I'm faced with the truth of it: They were stolen while I was inside the house.

But who would steal them? Who would steal them from *me*, the seventh son of the Supreme Overlord of the Universe?

Then it hits me. If what Kal said is true, maybe my father isn't the most powerful being in existence. If our universe is one of many, then there have to be many Supreme Overlords. That means lots of *sons* of Supreme Overlords. Maybe I'm not so special after all. I wonder if Dad knows about this. I shake my head. I can't focus on that now. Random theft is very rare in The Realms. Someone must have known I had these and followed me here.

But who? And why?

Annika squints at the labels on the two recovered dots. "Amino acids," she reads from one. "Cambrian explosion." She looks at me. "What does that mean?"

I shake my head, feeling utterly defeated. "I don't know," I tell her in a flat voice. "There were thousands of dots in that box. Without that information, there's no way to rebuild everything on Earth exactly the same as it was."

"Does it have to be exactly the same?"

I nod. "Everything has to lead up to you looking in the telescope. Only this time you can't look, or Earth will disappear all over again."

"Oh." She looks down at the tiny dots in her hands, then slips them back into her pocket. "Let's take good care of these, then."

"Two tiny glimpses into Earth's history won't help us at all."

"Well, there must be backups of the others, right?"

I shake my head. "We have data on every planet in the universe, habitable or not. That's trillions of trillions of planets, with thousands of data dots for each. We're already running out of storage space."

I can tell she's about to say something judgmental about the importance of backing things up but is holding back. Instead, she says, "We need to find really smart people, people who understand how things work. Aunt Rae told me your brothers are responsible for a lot of stuff to do with the—what did she call them? The terrestrial planets? The rocky ones?"

I nod grimly, not liking where this is heading.

"Well, can't they help?"

"Trust me, it's bad enough that I have to ask my brother Ty to get us into the Afterlives."

"But if they can help, then we—"

"I've got an idea!" I say, cutting her off. "We're going to the Afterlives, right?"

She nods.

"We can ask the people there, the scientists who studied all this stuff when they were alive. As long as they didn't die too recently, they shouldn't have disappeared yet."

She sizes me up. "Maybe you won't make such a bad partner after all. I'm still running the show, but—" She suddenly starts gasping. Her eyes widen in fear, and her hand instinctively reaches for her neck. I lean over and feel her hair. Almost completely dry!

I reach for the bucket and, without warning, dump it on her head.

She sputters and coughs, glaring at me as she fills her lungs with tiny molecules of oxygen.

I grin. That was just as much fun as I'd imagined.

> *The universe is full of magical things, patiently*
> *waiting for our wits to grow sharper.*
> — **Eden Phillpotts, writer**

12

he Afterlives are all the way at the far end of
The Realms, which means there is plenty
of opportunity for Annika to ask me a lot of
really annoying questions as we walk there.
*Why don't you have cars? How do you breathe? Are you really
immortal? Where ARE we? Why can I see outer space
beneath the ground? Why are there so many statues of
strange-looking people everywhere?*

Clearly Aunt Rae didn't have a chance to explain everything about The Realms. So now I get that fun task. When
Annika finally stops talking to take a breath, I begin to
answer. "Besides not having the materials to build them,
we don't have cars because there's no rush to get anywhere.
We don't experience time the way you do. Things here
don't..." I search for the right word. "They don't *decay* like
the rest of the universe. Or I guess they do, but so much
slower that it's not really noticeable. We don't need to

breathe because our bodies are made of the same stuff as the atmosphere around us. We don't have the same kind of lungs and blood that you do. We assume we're immortal because no one has ever died. My best friend, Kal, and his parents might be dying now, though, which is why I want to rebuild Earth as much as you do. Kal's parents were on the planet when it…well, you know, and now they're trapped in some other universe and Kal is stuck there with them. But if Earth comes back, they will, too." I sound more certain of that than I actually am. But I have to believe that or else I'll give up before I even begin.

She stops walking. "People from *here* came to Earth? You have spaceships but no cars?"

I shake my head. "No spaceships, either. We create what you'd call a wormhole through space and travel through it to the planets. A wormhole is when you pair a black hole, which sucks things in, with a white hole, which spits things out."

Eye roll. "I know what a wormhole is. Remember my dad? Big outer-space guy?"

A thought suddenly occurs to me, which is somewhat of a rare occurrence. "Hey, I bet that's how you wound up here! You probably got sucked into the wormhole left open for Kal's parents! You must have gone through it right before everything got pulled out of the space-time continuum. That's why you never disappeared like everyone else!"

She looks doubtful. "I never thought I'd say this, but if

I'm fortunate enough to get to listen to my dad talk for hours about the wonders of the universe again, I'll ask him if it's possible to create a wormhole big enough, or stable enough, to travel in. Because I'm pretty sure it's not."

I shrug. "We've had a lot longer than you to figure it out. Do you want me to keep answering your questions or not?" I turn off the street and we trudge through an open field full of tall grasses and even taller statues. The inhabitants of The Realms love making art, and Grayden's job is to inspire them to create it. This means that a lot of the statues have a decidedly Grayden-like appearance to them.

"This is a shortcut," I explain. Kal knows even better shortcuts, but I've only been to the Afterlives a few dozen times in my whole life. It's sort of a sacred place, a very private place where visitors are discouraged. Whenever someone dies, anywhere in the universe, a piece of their essence—a part of what makes them *them*—gets stored here. The rest goes somewhere else. No one knows where. Or if they do, they haven't told me.

"So let me get this straight," Annika says. "The Realms isn't a planet, it's...something else?" She ducks around a particularly large statue of a scaly two-headed Ojeron (who still, by the way, looks like Grayden, even with the extra head).

I hesitate. Since time began, knowledge of The Realms has been carefully hidden from all other inhabitants of the universe. We wouldn't be having this discussion right now if the Powers That Be didn't believe so strongly in keeping our secrets. Should I really be the one to reveal them?

Annika stumbles a bit and puts her hand on my arm to steady herself. "Sorry," she mumbles, reddening slightly.

One touch of her hand and I lose my train of thought. Embarrassing. Where was I? Oh right, explaining The Realms. "It's like this." I look down at my feet as I speak, trying to trick myself into believing that I'm talking only to myself. She simply happens to be close enough to overhear. "The Realms are inside what you call dark matter," I explain to my feet. "We fill up most of the space in the universe. The Realms are so enormous that no one has been to all of it. Parts of it reach out into all the galaxies. Our wormholes are more like really long elevators, so really, you don't have to leave The Realms to get anywhere else."

I glance up to see how she's taking all this. She's staring at me with wide eyes. I pick up my pace a bit and drop the pretense of not talking directly to her. If we're really in this together, she'll need to understand as much as possible. "As far as I know, The Realms have been here since the beginning of time, or near there, anyway. Nothing changes too much."

"It looks pretty different from yesterday," she points out.

I look around us. Everything has gone back to normal now, with the exception of a few scattered hot dog and ice cream stands. Those are harder to let go of. "I'm sure it was easier for you when things looked more like Earth and less like . . . well, like this."

She doesn't answer, only scrunches up her face in a way I can't interpret. I wish she could see the beauty of The

Realms, the glowing, pulsing heart of it. To her, the tall grass we're walking through must look like weeds, instead of living tendrils of light and shadow. The buildings and homes must look very flat, transparent, and boring, with only the occasional splashes of colorful art to break up the monotony. But the structures are an extension of ourselves, nearly alive in their own right.

I feel the need to defend my home. "You should know that The Realms don't really look like this," I tell her. "I mean, if you could see more than just the visible spectrum of light. Humans only—"

"And by *humans*, you mean me?" she says, her voice colder than I'd heard it.

"Um, I was talking about all humans. Your eyes can—"

"But I'm the only human now, aren't I?"

"I'll just stop talking," I mumble. Did I say too much? Too little? Girls are really hard to figure out.

"Are we almost there?"

"Almost." We continue walking in silence.

Annika's gasp startles me. I don't blame her for being surprised. We've reached the end of the field, and the Afterlives now loom before us. And boy, do they loom. The mirrored walls go up so high they disappear from view. The walls reflect back our surroundings, rendering the Afterlives practically invisible.

Annika waves her hand. Her reflection waves back. Annika sticks out her tongue. Her reflection does the same. This could go on for a long time. "Are you sure you want to go inside?" I ask, hoping to distract her from the wall. "It might not be what you expect."

Ignoring the question, she sticks two fingers in her mouth and pulls at the sides, giggling at her reflection. Then she abruptly turns away from the wall. "How come you didn't tell me I have cherry pie in my teeth? What kind of friend doesn't tell another friend when they have pie in their teeth?"

I step back. "Oh, we're friends now?"

"I thought we were starting to be," she says, picking out a barely visible piece of cherry skin from between two teeth. "Now I'm not so sure."

"I am deeply, deeply sorry," I say in an exaggerated apology. "Please find it in your heart to forgive me. I promise if you ever have food in your teeth I will tell you. Even if I can't see it, and I can see everything."

"That's all I ask," she says, sticking out her chin. "Now let's go see my grandfather before all traces of him disappear. He died only a few years before my grandmother, so according to Aunt Rae, he won't be around much longer."

My recent offense apparently forgiven, she follows me alongside the wall until we get to a small, shiny knob. If you weren't looking for it, you'd never notice it.

Up close it becomes more obvious that it isn't one straight wall, but rather dozens of connected buildings. Ty's office is behind the door marked SCENERY & DESIGN. I've only visited him here at work a couple of times ever, and never unexpectedly. The first time I came I was really young and a little confused. Were the people dead? Alive? Half-alive? Bren had to hold my hand the whole time but he never teased me about it afterward. Annika hesitates before following me inside. I don't blame her.

We find Ty staring at his view screens, his eyes flicking from one to the next. It might look like he isn't doing much of anything, but I know that's not true. It's his job to make sure everyone's Afterlife experience is as realistic and pleasing as possible. He and his staff are in charge of weather, accessories, food, and music. With all the differences, big and small, among the intelligent species, they have to make sure nothing gets messed up. You wouldn't want to feed a Senturon a chicken salad by mistake. All of it is generated by the holos, of course, but it's very real to the person (the essence of the person?) experiencing it.

I tap Ty on the shoulder. "Hi, Ty. This is Annika." He jumps out of his seat so fast the cap he always wears goes flying off. He grabs for it and glances up at Annika. "She's wetter than I'd have expected."

"Joss poured a bucket of water on my head," Annika says.

"That's not a very nice way to treat your guest, Joss," Ty scolds. "Do I need to tell Mom?"

I glare at Annika.

"That's for the pie in my teeth," she whispers.

I open my mouth to remind Annika that the water is keeping her alive, but she doesn't give me a chance. "I'd like to see my grandfather," she tells Ty. "If he hasn't disappeared from the Afterlives like my grandmother."

"This is highly unusual, Joss," Ty says sternly.

"I know." I reach into my pocket and pull out a folded piece of paper. "And I need you to sign this."

He takes the paper and begins to read. "I, Ty, third son of the Supreme Overlord of the Universe, do solemnly swear not to reveal anything about what I am about to hear."

He looks up. "What is this?"

"Keep reading."

He tosses the paper on his desk. "Joss, I don't have time for this. Sixteen million babies are about to be born in Sector Three alone. I have to make sure all the proud parents are in place and—"

"Please," Annika says, her voice barely restrained. "Can you just sign whatever it is so we can get a move on? I hear death isn't as permanent as it used to be."

Ty peers closely at Annika. He reaches out a finger and taps her on the top of the head. "Interesting." Then he does it again, a little slower this time.

She narrows her eyes at me. "Does anyone in your family understand the concept of personal space?"

"C'mon, Ty," I say, pushing the paper back into his hands. "Just sign this and then I'll explain. It was Gluck's idea."

"Fine," he grumbles, scribbling his name on the bottom

without even questioning the punishment for breaking the agreement—cleaning my room for the next millennia.

Annika and I watch as he presses some buttons and literally millions of tiny newborn babies howl in their parents' waiting arms. Some are pink, some brown, some orange, some have scales, some have tentacles, some are tiny, some are huge. A few even come out speaking full sentences. One begins to sing.

Apparently satisfied with his work, Ty hops back up from his desk. "So what can I help you with?"

Annika is glued to the screens. I have to call her name three times before she tears herself away.

"Well," I begin, "you know how Earth was taken out of time?"

He glances uncertainly at Annika.

"It's okay," she says. "I already know."

"Anyway, Gluck told me I have to bring it back. And I don't have the holofilms anymore and now I have to piece it all together from scratch. We're here to ask a famous Earth scientist how to do it."

"And to see my grandfather," Annika adds.

"*You?* You have to rebuild Earth?" Ty doesn't bother to hide his surprise. "Why you? No offense."

"None taken," I reply, and really, there isn't. "Maybe because everyone else is so busy?" I can't tell him what Gluck said, about picking me because I care the most about Kal and his parents. The fact that they are missing is still a secret. At least I think it is. It's getting hard to keep track!

Annika looks questioningly at me but doesn't say anything about Kal, which I appreciate. "And you know how Dad is," I add. "He'd never go back on his own decision, even if he wanted to."

Ty nods.

Annika pinches my arm.

"Ow! What was that for?"

"Your *father* destroyed my planet? I thought Aunt Rae said it happened on its own. Something about breaking the laws of physics?"

Ty takes this moment to suddenly find some vitally important papers to shuffle through at his desk. I'm beginning to think Aunt Rae conveniently left out the most important details so I'd get stuck explaining them.

"It wasn't my father's decision alone," I insist, finding myself in the odd position of having to defend him. "He's the head of the Powers That Be. You know, the guys in the suits and robes that all kinda look alike? They're just doing their jobs, trying to figure out what's best for everyone."

She takes a sharp breath. "How was making my planet disappear best for everyone who lived there? Earth was supposed to survive another five billion years before the sun burned out or the Milky Way collided with Andromeda or something. I want those five billion years back!"

I look to Ty for help but he doesn't even look up. Nice.

"Look," I tell her, anxious to be done with this conversation. "It's not like I don't agree with you. Obviously I do, or we wouldn't be here. But these are just the rules. Even the

101

PTB don't make the rules. Like you said, it's something to do with the fundamental laws of physics, and you broke them."

"Not on purpose!" she insists.

"Look, we're trying to fix this. Can we please focus on that part of it?"

She presses her lips together, but nods.

"Ty, can you please take us to Annika's grandfather now?"

He stands up and pulls a small holoscreen from his pocket. "Full name and last known address?" He holds the screen out and gestures for her to speak into it.

"Morty Klutzman," she says, louder than necessary. "Twenty West Shore Trail, apartment one C, Richford, Ohio."

Ty takes the screen back and flips through some entries. While we're waiting, Annika whispers, "Grandpa smelled like cigars and peppermints and soft flannel shirts. Will he still smell the same?"

"Sorry. I've never smelled anyone in the Afterlives before."

"Got him," Ty says, snapping his holoscreen shut. "Category One. Let's go."

"Category One?" Annika repeats. "What does that mean?"

Ty picks up his official "I'm someone important" badge and slips it over his neck. "It means he's still reliving his life, or his favorite parts, anyway. Once the deceased is here longer, they're usually ready to move on to Category Two."

"What happens in Category Two?" she asks. I'm glad she does, because I'm curious, too.

"That's classified," Ty says firmly. "Now let's go."

He walks over to a door that I always thought was a closet. Probably because of the word CLOSET written overhead in thick black letters. The "closet" turns out to be a narrow passageway, pulsing all around us with energy. The walls are so blindingly bright that I can barely see the tunnel winding endlessly ahead of us. We don't get farther than two feet before Annika bumps right into me.

"That should have hurt," she says, surprised, feeling her nose. "Why didn't that hurt?"

I really don't have the patience to explain about how we're made of more empty space than she is. So instead I step aside and say, "Will you be less likely to collide with me if you walk ahead of me?"

"I would be less likely to collide with you if someone turned on a light!"

"What are you talking about? There's so much light it's practically blinding."

Ty elbows me. "She can't see it, Joss. We're at the far end of the electromagnetic spectrum here, surrounded by gamma rays. I know school isn't your favorite thing, but honestly, don't you pay attention at all?"

"All right, all right," I reply, rubbing my arm angrily. It

might not have hurt her nose but it still hurt my arm. "I wasn't thinking. I've got a lot on my mind right now."

Ty turns away, but not before muttering, "Yeah, like how soon you can get back to Thunder Lanes to meet Kal."

Ty has never been one of my favorite brothers. He's always been a little curt and bossy. But I like him even less at this moment. I swallow back the many things that I really want to say, and put both hands on Annika's shoulders. "Come on, I'll guide you so you won't bump into anything."

Annika is silent as we shuffle through hallway after gleaming, shimmering hallway. It's a little weird gripping a girl's shoulder bones, but not entirely unpleasant.

"Is it cool?" Annika asks, over her shoulder.

"Is what cool?"

"How everything really looks, you know, if I could see it."

I don't want to make her feel bad, but there's no use lying. "Yes, it's pretty amazing. But to everyone in The Realms, it's just the way things are. The way they've always been."

"You're so lucky."

Ty snorts. "If you think *we're* lucky, you'd be really jealous of the five-eyed Zoren from the Southern Pinwheel Galaxy. Not only can he see the whole spectrum of electromagnetic energy, he can see in four dimensions and—"

Annika stops short. This time it's me who bumps into her. "The *who* from the *where*? Are you telling me that besides *this* place, there's life on other *planets*? And there are *four* dimensions?"

At this rate we will NEVER get anywhere. "Can we focus on one thing at a—"

WOO WOO WOO WOOOOOOO!!!!

The three of us jump and cover our ears. I've never heard this kind of siren before. It's different from the one that wailed when Annika witnessed Aunt Rae in the kitchen. After a few more bursts, the siren stops. Deafening shouts of "INTRUDER ALERT, INTRUDER ALERT" take its place.

"What are the odds they're not talking about us?" I yell to Ty.

"Not good," he yells back.

I'm about to tell Annika not to worry when a pair of large hands reach out from the wall and yank her right through it. The last thing I see is her mouth fall open in surprise before the wall swallows her up.

I rush over to the spot she was pulled through. It feels just like any other wall in The Realms, sort of softish, but not so soft you should be able to pull a human through it. Yet that's exactly what happened.

Before I can ask Ty what's going on, he shrugs and says, "Well, back to work, I guess. Thanks for stopping by."

Life is eternal and love is immortal; and death is only a horizon. And a horizon is nothing save the limit of our sight.

—Rossiter W. Raymond, writer, engineer

13

Ty, wait! You have to help me find Annika! If she dries, she'll die!" Ty continues strolling back to his office as though the first and only living human being to set foot in The Realms in the history of the universe hadn't just been snatched away before our eyes. "Ty! Dad will be really mad at all of us if we lose her!"

He finally stops. "Listen, Joss, I commend you for trying to help the girl. But face it, this isn't going to end well. Annika can't live here forever. Her planet is gone. Let her go, too."

I shake my head at him. "How can you say that? Your entire job is to take care of people—granted, they're dead, but still, you're so willing to just let her go?"

"I don't expect you to understand," Ty says. "You're too close to the situation."

"Can you just tell me where she is? Who took her?"

He looks both ways, then lowers his voice. "The task force that monitors the Afterlives probably took her. It wasn't personal. I'm sure they thought she had slipped out of one of the sims. That's short for simulations."

"I wasn't born yesterday, Ty. I know what the sims are."

"Well, every now and again someone will wander unexpectedly from his or her current simulation. I'm sure they'll return her when they realize their mistake."

"But what if she—"

A popping noise cuts me off.

"And here she is now," Ty says, stepping aside to allow a red-faced Annika to climb out of the wall. She's a little drier and a lot angrier, but otherwise seems unharmed.

"Seriously?" she asks. "Did I just get pulled through a *wall*?"

I figure that's a rhetorical question. "Are you okay? What happened?"

"I still can't see you," she says, pouting angrily.

Ty pulls out his holoscreen and holds it up. The screen provides a small circle of light. Compared with the light around us, it's like a candle in the face of a star, but it's enough to allow Annika to see our shapes at least.

She blinks as her eyes adjust. "Thank you. So anyway, this really big guy with really big hands and a head slightly too big for his body—no surprise there—pulled me into this empty white room, stared at me for a minute, mumbled something into one of those screens that you're holding, then pushed me back through the wall. And now I'm here."

"So pretty uneventful, you'd say?" Ty asks.

She stares at him. "If you call getting pulled through a wall without your permission uneventful."

He shrugs. "Sounds like any other day to me. But if you want to see your grandfather, we better get moving. Probably not much time left."

I can tell Annika has a lot more she'd like to say about the incident, but she presses her mouth into a firm line and nods. Ty leads us back in the direction we had been heading earlier. At least he keeps his holoscreen on so Annika can see where she's going this time.

After what seems like a really long time, he finally stops. "We're here."

Annika and I turn around in a circle. The passageway looks exactly the same as it always has. "Where?" she asks.

"Here." Ty presses his hand onto the wall, which instantly dissolves to reveal an outdoor wedding scene in the distance. The young bride and groom dance inside a circle of clapping guests. Laughter and the sound of clicking glasses fill the air, and it smells like what I'd expect summer on Earth to smell like. A mixture of wet dirt, flowers, and hot dogs. I turn around, expecting to see the now-familiar hallway behind me, but instead I find a small pond with wedding guests walking along the shoreline. Above me is a perfectly blue sky. And a sun! A real sun! Or at least it looks real. Blazing low in the sky, just like I always imagined a sun would do.

"Don't stare at it," Ty says, shaking his head. "Honestly, I really don't think you pay attention in school at all!"

I look away from the sun and notice I'm wearing a white suit and brown loafers. My left hand clutches a glass of dark brown liquid. I take a sip. Mmm...chocolate milk! Ty might be kind of obnoxious, but he truly is a master at his job. I've never been in a sim before, but everything looks and feels totally real.

Annika—now sporting a long pale blue dress and white heels and holding a paper fan—inhales sharply. "Where are we? How did we get here?"

"We haven't gone anywhere," Ty explains. "We're still in the Afterlives, inside our simulation of your grandfather's memories. If he wanted to, he could spend the rest of eternity reliving this day. Or at least that was the plan before his planet and all its inhabitants were doomed because one girl looked where she wasn't supposed to."

I elbow him in the side and whisper, "Not the time!"

Ty ignores me, but when he addresses Annika again his voice is kinder. "There he is now, dancing with his bride."

Annika turns, then lifts one foot to pull out a heel that had gotten stuck in the grass. It sinks right back in. With a grunt, she yanks off both shoes, sticks the paper fan inside one, and throws them over her shoulder. They land next to a strolling violinist who deftly steps over them. I'm reminded of when she tossed her coat to the ground and stomped on it. That seems so long ago now. Look at me, thinking in terms of time. Kal would be proud.

In stocking feet, Annika takes a few steps toward the dance floor. "That's my grandfather? He's so...young! But if he's the groom, then...Grandma's the bride? But Aunt Rae said she disappeared!" Annika lifts her long skirts and starts running toward the dancers. "Grandma!" she yells. "Grandma, it's me!"

Ty jumps in her way and holds up his hand.

"What is it?" she asks, exasperated. She leans around him so she can keep an eye on the dancers.

"That's not really your grandmother," Ty says.

Annika's attention snaps back. "I've seen old pictures. I know my grandmother when I see her and that's her."

I can tell by the way Ty's left eye has begun to twitch that he can't believe he has to explain something as basic as how the Afterlives work. "I'll try to make this as easy to understand as possible," he says slowly, like he's talking to a four-year-old. "This is your grandfather's sim, so everyone you see is created from his memory. He is the only real person here. And by real, I mean his *essence* is still here. His body, of course, isn't still alive. Following me?"

Annika's brows furrow in confusion. "So if I go up to my grandfather, he'll know who I am, but my grandmother won't?"

Ty shakes his head. "Neither of them will. Your grandfather is truly reliving his day exactly as he experienced it the first time. You won't be born for another forty years, so he doesn't know you yet. He will only return to his present self for a brief juncture as the sim gets reset for the next event." Ty pauses to grab a mini hot dog from a waiter's plate. I grab one, too, and pop it in my mouth. It melts in the perfect combination of warm dough and salty meat. Delicious!

Annika taps her foot. "And how long till that happens?"

Ty swallows and dabs at his mouth with a napkin. "In your time frame? Let's see." He cups his holoscreen carefully in his hands so no one in the sim will see it. "In about a kilosecond. You'll be able to talk to him then."

She gets ready to run again but Ty puts out his hand to stop her. "Wait. I said we still have a whole kilosecond."

"Well, how long is that?"

Ty looks thoughtful. "Let's see . . . if every time a human blinks, three hundred million billion attoseconds have passed, then—"

"Attoseconds?"

"You know, the time it takes light to travel the length of three hydrogen atoms. About a billionth of a billionth of a second. Isn't that how you tell time on Earth?"

"No! We use this." She holds up her arm. Then, seeing her watch has been replaced by a dainty pearl bracelet, she lets her arm drop. "Well, you know what I mean. Hours, minutes, seconds. That's about it."

"Oh. Then it's about sixteen minutes and forty seconds." Ty's screen beeps and he glances down to read the message. "I need to go attend to a small glitch in a new arrival's sim," he says, shoving the holoscreen back in his pocket. "Apparently in her sim it's supposed to rain pebbles, but instead we've got rotten fruit. Making quite a mess, to say nothing of the smell."

"How can it rain pebbles?" Annika asks me.

"The planet she comes from must be very close to its sun. If the ground is molten, it would rain tiny pebbles instead of water droplets like on your planet."

"You're making that up. There's no—"

Ty cuts her off. "Stay out of the way until I get back. The Afterlives have rules even I don't know about. I'm sure we're breaking at least a dozen of them by being here and I have no idea what would happen if you were to interact with anyone, especially your grandfather. Please do not repay my kindness by trying to find out. Dad will get me demoted to stable detail on Orion Five." He shudders at the thought.

"But Ty, wait," I say, stepping forward. "What if Annika dries off? Is the water in that pond real?"

Worry crosses Annika's face and she quickly reaches up to feel her hair. "It's totally dry!"

"Don't worry," Ty replies. "Just like the people and the food, we replicate the water in the sims. But you won't need it because the molecules in the air are real, too. You can breathe in all the oxygen you want. For slightly less than a kilosecond longer, that is."

"Oh," Annika says, inhaling deeply. She lets it out slowly and smiles. "Cool."

He turns to leave again, but this time it's Annika who stops him. "Wait! What if my grandfather disappears before this simulation or whatever you call it ends?"

Ty glances at the dance floor, then shrugs. "We'll hope for the best." With a quick salute, he points to a recently vacated bench by the pond, takes one step backward, and disappears.

Annika shivers. "I'll never get used to that." We head over to the bench and sit. Annika positions herself so she can still watch her grandparents. They are now feeding each other pieces of yellow cake and laughing. "Okay, Joss, I'm giving you fair warning. If I'm not distracted really well, I'm going up there no matter what might happen to your brother. Cleaning stables might be good for him."

"Trust me, the stables on Orion Five aren't anything you'd wish on your worst enemy. The smell alone would take a few hundred years to wash off."

Annika stands up.

I pull her back down. Ty may not be my favorite, but no one deserves that fate. And he did bring us here, so I owe it to him to make sure we follow his rules. "All right, all right. How should I distract you? My juggling skills are subpar at best."

She shrugs innocently, a gesture I've learned to fear. "How about you explain the whole life-on-other-planets thing?"

I was afraid she'd ask about that. "I can turn my legs into wheels," I suggest. "Want to see that instead?"

She shakes her head. "I'll take you up on that sometime, but this probably isn't the place."

Good point. That would definitely bring us the type of attention Ty warned us against. My only hope may be to stall her until the sim is over. "Well, what do you know about life on other planets already?"

"Only what my dad's told me," she says. "I know astronomers have found lots of planets around other stars, and I know the planets have to be the right distance from their sun so the water doesn't boil away or freeze. They'd go crazy if they knew about The Realms. Now tell me, who else is out there?"

I hesitate. The people of Earth have only taken the first baby steps toward exploring space and understanding how to use the materials available to them. They are ahead of a lot of civilizations, but really, REALLY far behind others. Some have figured out how to use the natural resources available on their planets, like humans have, but others can harness the entire energy output of their sun, or their entire galaxy, or have left their home planet long ago. "Just so you know," I finally say, "I'm really not supposed to tell you anything. We can't interfere too much with primitive civilizations."

She bristles. "*Primitive?* It's not like we've only recently invented the wheel! We've walked on the moon! We have antibiotics and computer chips as small as a grain of sand! We have video games where your body is the controller! Really! You just stand in front of it and—"

"Okay, okay, maybe *primitive* was a bad choice of words. You're more like, not advanced?"

"That's just saying the same thing, only slightly nicer! And how can you say you don't interfere too much? You destroyed a perfectly good planet! Sure, we had our problems, but seriously, to pull us out of time? Who does that?"

I hold up my hands. "Again, that was not our fault." I stop short of saying it was *her* fault.

"But I don't understand why it had to happen at all," she says. "Why does it matter what I saw? No one would have believed me if I told them. They would have thought I had been dreaming, or was making it up."

It's no use telling her I'd already argued her case and lost. "My dad would say it's the natural order of things. *An action has a necessary reaction.* The planets aren't supposed to know about The Realms. Maybe the whole universe would come apart if Earth had been allowed to survive."

"Then why would Gluck be telling you to rebuild it?"

I lean back and shake my head. I've been asking myself that, too. I have no answer for her, so I watch the ducks go by in the pond. They've sure got it easy. Just bobbing along on the gentle current. Float, spread wings, nuzzle another duck, quack, then repeat. Pretty much what my life used to be like, I guess. Minus actually nuzzling any ducks.

"Sounds like the Powers That Be know they made a mistake," Annika mutters. "And want *you* to fix it for them."

I force myself to turn from the calm routine of the ducks. "The PTB don't make mistakes."

Annika harrumphs in response. Loudly. A few wedding guests turn to look. She gives them a tiny wave and they move on.

I lower my voice. "Hey, I'm the one who wanted to get Kal back any way possible. I would have done something even if Gluck hadn't asked me to. If you and I are going to work together, we're going to have to agree to disagree on whether or not what happened to your planet was necessary."

"Fine," she grumbles. "Just tell me about the other planets, then, because that cake is looking really good, and I might just go help myself to some."

The sound of drumbeats, low and steady and familiar, seems to rise up through the bench. "Kal?" I ask, jumping up and turning in circles. "Is that you? Kal? I'm in the Afterlives! Can you hear me?"

Annika pulls me back down. "Joss! I'm pretty sure you're not supposed to announce where we are." She looks around to make sure no one heard my outburst. "You said Kal's trapped somewhere....Is he trapped here? In my grandfather's simulation?"

A three-piece band under a white gazebo starts to play a

dance tune. Any drumbeats there might have been are drowned out. I don't answer right away, hoping the drumming will come back. "I'm not sure where he is," I finally say, "but I know he's trying to reach me. I'm not supposed to talk about it."

"Well, between the two things you're not supposed to talk about, how about you pick one?"

After one last listen, I give up on the drums. If Kal can find me here, he can find me anywhere. "Okay, if you must know, life exists somewhere in almost every galaxy in the universe. The same atoms and elements that made you made the creatures that live on those other planets."

She absorbs this news, then asks, "So they all look like us, then?"

"You know I don't really look like you, right?"

She tilts her head at me. "Well, there's the thing with the head being slightly too big, and those nonexistent pores, and you're a little squishy, but..."

"*Squishy?* I'm not squishy!"

She shrugs. "Whatever. Just keep going."

"I'm *not* squishy," I mutter. "Maybe a little *softish*, but that's not the same thing. Moving on. Yes, some advanced life-forms look like humans. Most have jointed limbs and hard skeletons. But life takes very different paths on each planet, depending on how close the planet is to its sun or other energy source, what the atmosphere is made of, how weak or strong the gravity is, the size and weight of the planet, how often it gets hit by asteroids, if it has a magnetic field, or a moon that affects its orbit and rotation. And a ton of other factors, like if the liquid on the planet is water or ammonia or methane or sulfuric acid or, well, you get the drift. That's why it's going to be so hard to rebuild your planet. There are so many things to get right. Or, more likely in our case, *wrong*. The interesting thing is, as soon as life could start on any planet, it did."

Annika shakes her head. "If that's all true, then how come no aliens have ever come to Earth?"

It feels strange to have someone asking me questions without doubting that I know the answer. I kind of like it. It almost makes me feel useful. "The universe is really huge," I explain. "I mean, really, really huge. It takes a long time to get anywhere. You're limited by the speed of light, too. I mean, you might find other planets with life on them, but when you look through your telescope, you're seeing them like they were hundreds, or even millions, of years earlier, depending on how long it takes light to reach them from where you are. And they'd see your planet the same way. If they were far enough away, they'd see dinosaurs when they looked at Earth, not humans. Here in The Realms, we aren't restricted by the speed of light. We can't go faster than it, of course, but we can see things as they actually are, everywhere at once."

"And then you can just travel anywhere you want with your supermagic wormholes?"

I smile. "They're not magic. It only seems that way."

"Have *you* ever seen an alien?"

"I'm looking at one right now."

"Where?" She whirls around in her seat.

I laugh. "Right next to me."

She points to herself. "*Me?* I'm not an alien!"

"To everyone outside of Earth you are."

"I never thought of it that way," she says as we watch the crowd gather to throw rice at the bride and groom. "Hey, how much time do we have left?" Without waiting for my answer, she jumps up. "C'mon!" She grabs my arm and tries to pull me toward the action. I do not budge.

"Suit yourself," she says, striding away with her dress swishing behind her.

Nice. And after I told her all that stuff about aliens. I'll remember this. Seeing no choice, I try to look casual as I stride toward the wide tree she is using as cover. I guess I can't really blame her for wanting a closer look.

"Before you yell at me," Annika says when I reach her, "you don't have to worry, I'm not going to bother them. They just look so happy. I wonder how many times he's relived this day."

"Eleven hundred and six times," Ty says, appearing behind us. Annika jumps, but relaxes when it becomes clear he's not going to yell at her for getting so close.

"No matter what other important events happened in their lives," he continues, "or amazing trips or accomplishments, it's the weddings and births they request the most.

And the grandchildren. Humans are very taken with their grandchildren."

Annika smiles at him, and he flashes a quick smile in return, showing his soft side for the first time. We watch as Annika's grandparents climb into the back of a fancy gray car. They wave out the window as their friends and families shout and hoot. From the safety of the tree, Annika and I wave, too.

"And we're out," Ty says. Abruptly, the sim ends. We're in our regular clothes in a large white room, empty except for the comfortable armchair that Annika's grandfather—now white-haired and plump—is sitting on. The smile on his face stretches from ear to ear as he, no doubt, recalls his day. Then he sees us, and his jaw drops. He jumps up and hurries over. "Annika! Is that you?"

Her eyes fill with tears. "Hi, Grandpa!" She flings herself into his arms. They hug tight, and then he pulls back to look at her.

"You're so beautiful! So grown up!" Then he puts his hands to his head like it suddenly hurts. "But wait, if you're here, does that mean you're . . . oh no! Are you . . . have you passed on? Your parents! They must be beside themselves with grief!" He wobbles, and Annika quickly reaches out to steady him.

"It's nothing like that," she assures him. "I'm still totally alive."

Grandpa Klutzman turns to my brother. "I . . . I don't understand. How is this poss—"

He is cut off by a sharp wheezing sound from Annika, followed by two quick gasps as her eyes roll back in her head. I catch her before she hits the floor, then lay her down gently as Ty runs out of the room.

It's probably a good thing Mom never let us have a plant. We'd always forget to water it.

The vastness of the heavens stretches my imagination—stuck on this carousel my little eye can catch one-million-year-old light. A vast pattern—of which I am a part.

—Richard P. Feynman, physicist

14

This time it isn't quite as funny watching Annika cough and sputter as she begins to breathe again. Maybe because it took what seemed like a long time for Ty to bring the water (he had to scoop it out of a fountain in a nearby sim). Or maybe because Annika's grandfather had faded away as he'd held her hand. His shouts of "Come back to us, Annika! Come back!" still ring in my ears.

I help her sit up. She shakes out her arms, and water droplets fly through the air. "Ugh! This is getting old." She pushes her wet hair away from her face. "Where's Grandpa?" Before we can answer she's on her feet, dashing to the four corners of the room, then checking behind the armchair as though he might be hiding there. "Did his next sim start already and he had to go?"

Ty shakes his head. "He's gone for good."

Annika bursts into tears. "I didn't get to ask him anything! Or tell him about Sam, who was born the year after Grandpa died. And he probably thought *I* died just now and he'll never know that I just needed oxygen and I wanted to warn him that he was going to be pulled out of time and now he's gone!" She curls into a ball on the armchair and buries her face in her hands.

I look over at Ty, who motions for me to go over to her. "I didn't do too well the last time she was crying," I protest.

"I don't care," he says, pushing me. "There's no crying in the Afterlives! This is a happy place! You have to make her stop or it will upset all the people in their sims!"

"Fine," I snap. "You don't need to yell at me."

"Happy place!" he hisses again as I head over to her.

I put my hand on her shoulder, then lift it off, then place it back again. "Um, Annika? If it makes you feel any better, I'm sure your grandfather knew you were going to be okay."

"Did you tell him?" she asks between sniffles.

I look up at Ty, who glares at me. I really don't want to lie, but I guess in this case it's for the greater good. "Um, yeah, he knew, don't worry."

She sniffles again, and wipes her nose on her arm before sitting back up. "Thanks, Joss. That does make me feel better."

I try to steer the topic away from my lie. "And at least he got to see you and hug you. No one else in the history of the Afterlives has ever been able to do that."

Ty nods in confirmation.

I hold out my hand. "C'mon, let's go find that scientist."

She nods, wipes her eyes once more, and takes my hand. As soon as she stands, we quickly let our hands drop apart. I pick up the extra bucket of water my brother had the foresight to bring back with him, glad to have something else to do with my hand. Ty touches the wall and we're back in the hall again.

"Oh, great," Annika says. "I'm blind again."

"One last stop," Ty warns us as he flips open his holoscreen so Annika can have some light. "I can't give tours of the Afterlives all day. And if there's any more crying, I'm tossing you both out."

"Don't look at me," I say. "I don't think we have tear ducts."

"There won't be," Annika promises.

"Which scientist did you want to visit?" Ty asks.

"Carl Sagan," she answers without hesitation. "He's my dad's favorite astronomer. We even named our cat Sagan. His full name is Sagan BB Klutzman."

"What does the BB stand for?" I ask.

"*Billions and billions*, obviously. You know, Carl Sagan's catchphrase?"

I shake my head. "I have to study famous people from a million planets, remember? My favorite catchphrase is 'Never turn your back on a Niffum in the rain.'"

Ty shudders. "Man, ain't *that* the truth."

"I'll keep that in mind if I ever run into a Niffum," Annika says drily. "And yours isn't even a catchphrase—it's more like *advice*. But Carl Sagan? He's like, the coolest astronomer in the world. There's an asteroid named after him, and also a piece of land on Mars where the first rover touched down. He made all these important discoveries and was really involved with the search for life on other planets."

"I thought you weren't interested in stuff like that," I say. "You said your dad was the one dragging you outside with the telescope."

"I never said I didn't like it," she insists. "Just maybe not as much as my dad." Her face lights up as she talks about her father. "When he was young, he saw this television special that Carl Sagan made. That's what got him interested in outer space in the first place. He really loved teaching me and Sam all that stuff."

Her face clouds over as she thinks about her family.

Ty punches the name into his holoscreen. "It was your father's telescope you were looking through when you spotted Aunt Rae baking her apple pie, right?"

"Yes."

"So what you're basically saying, then, is that Carl Sagan is to blame for your planet being gone."

"What? I...no way...I mean...he would never... I..."

"Just ignore my brother," I tell Annika, patting her arm.

"No one was to blame, least of all the guy you named your cat after."

"That's right," she says, stomping one foot for emphasis. "Hey, wait, what happened to my cat when the world ended? And everyone else's pets?" Her eyes start to well up.

Ty can't see her cry! I turn her to face me and say firmly, "Your world didn't end. As it stands now, your world never was. Sagan BB Klutzman never existed. And soon neither will the other Sagan, so we have to hurry if we want to talk to him."

Ty leans over, suspicious. Annika blinks quickly to dry her eyes. "Sorry," she says. "I'm fine, really."

"I found your guy, so keep it together." He leads us down another passageway, and then another. I'm beginning to get an idea of how enormous the Afterlives are. I keep checking to make sure Annika hasn't dried out. I feel better having the water with me. I keep one ear out for Kal's drums, but the hallways are totally silent. There is no indication of all the sims being lived out on either side of us.

"We're here," Ty says, finally stopping.

This time we don't ask where here is, we just wait for him to let us into the sim. Instead he just leans against the wall and says, "We don't have long to wait."

"You're not going to let us in?" Annika asks.

Ty shakes his head. "It was different for your grandfather because you didn't know if he'd hang around long enough to talk to, but in this case why watch someone you can't interact with? His sim will be over shortly, and then you can talk to him. My records show he passed away a number of years before your grandfather, so he's not going to disappear before you get your time with him. Have a little patience."

I haven't known Annika too long, but I'm pretty sure patience isn't one of her strong suits.

"But if we went inside," Annika argues, "we could learn something important. Maybe he's in the middle of teaching an astronomy class!"

"Okay, that's unlikely," Ty says. "But you're going to drive me crazy if I don't let you in, aren't you?"

"Oh, totally," she says.

"Fine," he grumbles. "Just stay in the background like last time and I'll meet you after the sim ends."

The wall dissolves and we find ourselves in the middle of a small, cozy library. Long wooden shelves full of books line the walls, children's colorful drawings hang above them, and a handful of families mill about, browsing or reading. Not exactly the university classroom we'd been hoping for. I don't see anyone who looks like a scientist. Not that I know what one would look like other than what I've seen on the view screens. I look around for an old guy in a white lab coat with messy hair and deep thoughts.

The sound of weeping fills the room. Annika and I turn toward the source—a young boy, no more than five or six years old. He's sitting on a metal folding chair in the corner of the children's section, hunched over a large picture book. His legs swing back and forth, too short to reach the ground. His small frame shakes with his tears.

I know before it happens that Annika is going to try to comfort the boy. I could stop her from hurrying over to him, but I don't. I just follow. None of our brief interactions with the simulated characters in her grandfather's sim seemed to matter. So until Dr. Sagan himself comes along, I don't really see the harm.

"Are you all right?" Annika asks, kneeling down beside him. "Are you lost? Do you need me to find your mommy?"

He shakes his head and looks up from his lap. Both Annika and I take a step back. His eyes shine so bright, they seem to glow from within. And it's not from the tears. I recognize his expression. It is one of unimaginable wonder, of pure joy. I've seen it on the faces of the people Kal brings to the Afterlives, when they get their first true glimpse of The Realms and the expanse of the universe around them. No longer confined by their limited senses, they often break down and weep.

The little boy points to the book on his lap and we step closer again. The page is open to a picture of the Milky Way Galaxy. Not bothering to wipe away the tears still flowing down his red, shiny cheeks, he says, "Did you know that the stars...all the stars we see around us...they're all SUNS?" He taps the picture with his finger. "That's a sun." Another tap. "And that's a sun." Tap. "And that's a sun." Tap tap tap. "They're ALL SUNS! All *billions and billions* of them!"

I guess we've found who we're looking for. I reach to pull Annika away but she shakes off my arm. "Wow, billions and billions!" she says, still kneeling beside him. "That's really amazing!"

The young Carl Sagan beams. "I know! And around those suns, there could be a planet like ours. And to them, our sun would just be another tiny dot in the sky!" He turns the pages of his book. "The universe is soooooo big! There's so much to learn!" Fresh tears fill his eyes as he shakes his head. He must have missed the message about not crying in the Afterlives.

I clear my throat. We're doing exactly what we promised Ty we wouldn't. "Um, we really have to go now," I tell the boy. "Are you sure you don't want us to find your mother?"

He shakes his head.

Ignoring me, Annika tells him, "Don't worry about all the things you don't know yet. You'll have a lot of years to learn this stuff. Something tells me you're going to be a great astronomer. The best! You're going to inspire a lot of people."

I stare at her, incredulous, but she doesn't turn away from the boy.

He beams up at her again, then asks, "What does *inspire* mean?"

Now *her* eyes are welling up. She kneels down again and

says, "It means that your enthusiasm, your *love* for science and the universe, is going to make a lot of people want to learn more about it. And the more people know about how the universe works and how we came to be here, the more we'll be able to connect with each other and our planet. You'll keep everyone reaching for the stars."

"*Me?*" he asks, bouncing up and down so fast I'm afraid he's going to fall off the chair. "I could be a scientist? You really think so?"

"I really do." She pats him on the knee and stands up, looking pretty pleased with herself.

"Where'd you get *that* speech from?" I whisper.

"Guess some of what my father said sank in after all."

The young Carl jumps up and runs right past us. He throws himself into the arms of his mother, nearly knocking over the pile of books she's carrying into the room. While he tells her about all the stars being suns, I take the opportunity to steer Annika behind a tall bookshelf before she goes up and introduces herself to his mother, which I would not put past her at this point.

"Okay, seriously?" I ask, to borrow one of her own favorite catchphrases. "Remember what Ty said before? Even *he* doesn't totally understand how the Afterlives work. You could have just changed the whole course of this guy's life. You weren't there the first time he found that book. What if he would have turned out to be a truck driver, or a veterinarian, or a chef, and it was because of you that he didn't?"

She grins. "Then everyone would thank me."

"I don't think Ty will thank you."

"You worry too much," she says, which is totally untrue. I can hardly remember worrying about much of anything before those sirens wailed at Kal's house.

"C'mon, Joss. This is just a simulation, right? It's not like one of those science fiction stories where a character travels back in time and then when they get back to the present everything's different because of something they did in the past. We didn't travel anywhere."

"I guess you're right. The Afterlives work in weird ways, though. We probably shouldn't mention it to Ty."

"Agreed," she says, only half paying attention. She's busily scanning the books on the nearest shelf. She pulls out one titled *Earth from A to Z*. "Quick," she says, "grab some more! Maybe Ty will let us take them with us!"

That's actually a great idea. I pull book after book off the shelf. *The Solar System and You. Single-Celled Organisms. Asteroids and Comets: Friends or Foes?*

"The sim is going to end really soon," I tell her. "Let's take what we have and get ready for Ty."

We gather the books into two stacks. She hands me the bigger pile and says, "Nice outfit, by the way."

I notice for the first time that I'm wearing long plaid shorts, knee socks, and brown loafers. Also a white button-down shirt and a blue blazer. Annika has on the same outfit, except instead of shorts she's wearing a pleated skirt. I look superdorky, but somehow she carries it off.

One of her books slips off the pile and falls open. She

reaches for it, glances at the page it fell open to, and frowns. "These books aren't going to help us much."

"Why? Because they're old?"

"No," she says, holding it up to me. "Because they're blank."

I stare at the white, empty pages, deflated. "Figures. I guess only the book your young friend needed has actual pages."

As we begin reshelving the books the sim dissolves, leaving us in a small white room, identical to the first except without the armchair. Annika, still damp I'm happy to see, is back in the clothes she got from Aunt Rae. I look down at our empty hands. Guess the books wouldn't have come with us anyway. Ty steps through the wall into the room. "How'd it go?"

"Fine," I say, maybe a tiny bit too quickly.

"Anything unusual to report?" he asks.

"Nope," Annika replies. "Same old, same old."

"Good," he says. "Because the guest of honor has arrived."

We turn to see Carl Sagan, the gray-haired grown-up version, rise from the metal folding chair that I'm sure wasn't there when we arrived. He is still short, and slight, and his eyes are as bright and his smile as wide as when he was a child. Ty steps forward to introduce us.

"No need, no need," he says. "I've been waiting to see this young lady again for a long time." And with that, he grabs Annika and pulls her into a tight bear hug. She flashes Ty a sheepish grin.

"Nothing unusual happened in the sim, eh?" Ty asks, narrowing his eyes at me.

I widen my eyes and try to look innocent. "Maybe he's just superfriendly?"

Dr. Sagan begins to swing Annika around while shouting, "It's you, it's you, it's really you!"

Ty shakes his head. "No one's *that* friendly."

15

Ty steps forward, holding up his official badge. "Sir, I'm going to have to ask you to stop spinning the girl."

Dr. Sagan slows, then stops.

Ty directs his attention toward Annika. "Would you care to explain why this esteemed astronomer, whom you've supposedly never met, seems so fond of you?"

Annika shrugs guiltily. "Some people just take an instant liking to me."

"Not all of them," I assure her.

Ignoring my comment, she says, "It's a curse sometimes, really. The responsibility that comes with being so widely adored. I tell you, it is *not* easy."

Ty rolls his eyes. "Dr. Sagan, would you care to take a better shot at an explanation?"

"Call me professor," he replies, holding out his hand for Ty to shake. "It reminds me of the eager faces of my students at Cornell." He starts reciting a poem. "'As you set out for Ithaka, hope the voyage is a long one, full of '—"

A stern look from Ty cuts him off.

"All right, all right, no poetry. How wonderful is it to be here! How lucky I am to get to relive the moment the enormous scale of the universe first revealed itself to me. And on the very day I met the girl who told me I could be a scientist!" He makes a move to hug Annika again, but Ty holds up his hand.

"I'm sorry, the girl who what?"

Annika tries to make herself look smaller by slumping and lowering her head. It does not work. I take Ty by the arm and pull him aside. "Okay," I whisper, "I know this looks bad, but Professor Sagan's going to disappear soon anyway, so whatever unintended consequences came from Annika's meddling in the sim won't matter for much longer. Please let us use the time we have left to get some answers. I'll owe you one."

Ty glances over at Annika and Sagan, now talking and laughing like old friends. "Fine," he snaps, turning back to me. "Do what you need to do to rebuild Earth and get the residents of the Afterlives back where they belong. That's how you can repay me."

"I'll try my best. I promise."

He looks me straight in the eye. "You know you'll never be able to do this, right?"

I swallow hard. "I can't think that way. I have to believe I can."

"Your job is to deliver pies, little brother, not rebuild solar systems."

"Don't you think I know that? Thanks for the support."

"I'm sorry, Joss," he says, heading for the nearest wall. "I'm trying to be realistic so you don't get your hopes up." Without saying good-bye to the others, he slips through the wall. I guess we're on our own.

Professor Sagan begins laughing at something I didn't hear. It's a loud, hearty, joyous laugh. Annika hesitates only briefly, then starts laughing, too. The two of them are laughing so hard it's impossible not to join in. The three of us laugh and laugh, and it feels good, like I'm laughing the worry out of my body. Eventually I choke out, "Why are we...ha ha ha...laughing?"

The professor dabs his eyes with his sleeve, and slowly regains himself. "Ah, that felt good. We were laughing because of something dear Annika said. Go on, tell him."

Annika's laugh peters out into giggles, then a chortle, then a hiccup. When she finally composes herself, she says, "Um, it's actually not all that funny. I asked him how we would rebuild Earth exactly the way it was. You know, if for some reason it got destroyed, or like, taken out of time or something."

"And?" I prompt.

"Well, that's when he started laughing."

"Oh. You're right. That's not so funny."

"Come now, young man," Professor Sagan says. "Don't look so down. I didn't know you were serious. Why would anyone need to rebuild Earth?" Then he looks startled. "We haven't gone and blown ourselves up, have we?"

"No, no," Annika assures him. "It's more that, well..." She trails off.

Clearly she's having a hard time telling him the truth. He's going to disappear any minute, why does it really matter now? So I blurt out, "It's because Earth has been taken out of time and we have to put it back exactly how it was before Annika saw Aunt Rae with the pie so that everyone comes alive again and people stop disappearing from the Afterlives."

The professor grabs the back of the chair for support. "Taken out of time? Everyone's gone from Earth? From here?"

Annika's eyes widen and she gives me a quick shake of her head.

"Um, uh." I scramble to find the right words. "Not for real, of course, I mean. It's a project we're doing for school. Extra credit."

"That's right." Annika jumps in. "Joss here got in trouble for not paying attention and this is the only way he'll pass his Planet Building class."

"Way to oversell it," I mutter.

"Ah, I see!" the professor says, brightening. "Phew! I'd be happy to help with your project. Anything for a friend of Annika's."

I force myself to let that go without comment, although it's difficult. "Thank you," I say instead. "Let's start at the beginning. What would we do first?"

The professor begins to pace the small room, a bounce in his step. I think he's happy to have students again.

"All right, first we need to establish what you mean by the beginning. Is it when primordial dust and gas left over from the sun first clumped together to form Earth? Or once the first microorganisms filled the oceans of our water-covered planet? Or once the growth of blue-green algae created enough oxygen to fill the air and give rise to more complex life?"

Annika and I exchange a look. "Those are a lot of long words," she replies. "But actually it's more like the whole solar system. Where we have to start from, I mean."

His brows rise. "That's certainly an ambitious project. Your friend here must need a lot of extra credit."

"But it's possible?" Annika asks with a hopeful tilt of her head.

Professor Sagan begins to pace again. "Let's see. So your goal is to rebuild our solar system so that life arises and evolves exactly the same way that it did the first time—your new planet will be the same size and weight, be the same exact distance from the sun, with a moon the size and location of ours, correct?"

We nod.

"And of course you'd put Jupiter in exactly the right

place to protect the young Earth from constant bombardment by comets and asteroids?"

"Of course," Annika replies. "Can't forget something as important as Jupiter."

He continues pacing. "And every single one of your direct ancestors will live long enough to have a child, until eventually, four and a half billion years after the planet formed into a sphere capable of one day supporting life, Annika Klutzman, the apple of her parents' eyes, will be born in the small midwestern town of Richford, Ohio?"

Annika looks a little less confident. "Um, yes?"

"Well, in that case . . ." Professor Sagan shakes his head. "Nope, sorry, totally impossible. If I were you, I'd ask your teacher if you could do something on a smaller scale. Turning a potato into a clock always wins big at school science fairs."

When neither of us replies, he says, "I could show you how to make a tiny volcano erupt using baking soda and vinegar. A little messy, but educational and fun at the same time."

"Thanks," I say, "but we really need to try this one first. The volcano can be plan B."

He puts his hand on my shoulder. "I admire your ambition, young Realms dweller, but there are so many steps to follow. First of all, you'd have to create the sun, and to do that you'd have to create the earlier stars, the ones that went supernova so the heavier elements they ejected into space will get absorbed into our sun. Without those, no rocky planet, no life. Only hydrogen and helium. You can't make people out of the primordial elements."

I clear my throat.

"Oh, sorry!" he says. "Present company excluded, of course."

"So we make the sun," Annika says. "Then what?"

"Well, then you'd take the dust and gas left over, allow it to clump together for about two hundred million years, until it makes one giant rock with an iron core. Then hurl another really big rock into your new planet so the pieces can fly off to form the moon. Without the moon, Earth would be unstable and its climates too severe for any complex life to survive. And make sure to tilt your planet's axis exactly twenty-three and a half degrees so you'll get the seasons."

"Seasons, got it. What's next?" Annika prompts.

He shakes his head at her, clearly amused by her unwillingness to give up, but continues. "You'll need movable tectonic plates, of course, to keep a steady supply of nutrients at the surface. And don't forget the oceans. You'd have to fill them. Take some water-bearing comets, add some volcanoes, and the atmosphere will start to fill with water vapor. Then here come the rains! And once you have water, and much later breathable oxygen, then—"

I know time is relative and all that, but his is surely running out. "Sir, I'm sorry to interrupt, but I'm sure you've seen all the galaxies and planets now that you've been in The Realms awhile, right?"

"Indeed I have," he says, his eyes glowing again. "The wonder of it all! The sheer number of planets harboring life. More than I ever would have guessed." He lowers his voice and whispers to Annika, "You should see some of the folks here in the Afterlives. Pretty bizarre."

"Really?" Annika asks, lowering her own voice.

"Can we focus, please?" I ask. "You can tell her about the purple-toed, three-eyed, five-armed Gordomorph later, okay?"

"Of course, of course." He winks at Annika and gestures with his hands like he's making an elephant's trunk from his nose.

Annika giggles.

Forging ahead, I say, "Even though my grade was less than stellar, I did learn a few things in Planet Building class. What you just told us could describe how almost all the terrestrial planets out there are made. What I really need to know are the specifics—the exact chemicals that are in the ground, in the air, in the people. How far exactly Earth and the other planets are from the sun. How and when life began there. Basically the details that make Earth different from all the other planets. I had this information, and then, well, I lost it." I can't bring myself to admit the data dots were stolen. It's still hard for me to accept.

As I wait for his answer, I notice a subtle shift in his

appearance. He doesn't seem as solid. I glance at Annika, but her expression hasn't changed. She can't see it. I turn back to the professor. The colors have now leeched from his clothes, his eyes, his skin. This is how it happened with Annika's grandfather. Sagan and I lock eyes. He knows something is wrong. His eyes flicker from panic to surprise, to understanding, to determination.

He digs into the pockets of his trousers and pulls out a small black tape recorder. It looks so old-fashioned and primitive, but it was probably the height of technology in his day. He also pulls out a small notebook held together by a rubber band. He hands the notebook to Annika, along with a pen. "Here, sweetheart. Why don't you number each page from one to twenty." He motions for her to sit in his folding chair. "Then I'll tell you and your friend what you need to know, okay?"

"Great," she says, undoing the rubber band.

He watches her wistfully, like a proud grandparent. "I'm really glad I got to know you," he tells her, his now-almost-colorless eyes shiny with more than just his usual enthusiasm.

She smiles up at him. "We named our cat after you."

The professor turns away to wipe his eye as she begins to write in the notebook. He beckons for me to follow him to the other side of the room. I know he is trying to keep her busy so she won't notice what's happening to him. His kindness at protecting her forms a knot in my throat. I don't know what to do. I want to get the information from him, but this is all happening so fast.

"I don't have long, do I?" he asks me, his voice low.

I shake my head. No use keeping it from him now.

"You're not really doing this for extra credit, are you?"

I shake my head again. He is now not much more solid than one of our hologram projections.

"Get it back, okay?" He reaches for my arm. His grip feels no stronger than a breeze. "Earth's atmosphere is seventy-eight percent nitrogen, twenty-one percent oxygen, and a pinch of argon, carbon dioxide, and water vapor." He says this firmly, as though focusing on facts and figures will ground him here in the Afterlives. I glance at Annika. She is still hunched over, still dutifully numbering the pages. She can't hear him anymore. His voice has faded to a range humans can't pick up.

"The outer layer of Earth," he continues, balling up his fists in determination, "is mostly made of only eight of the ninety-two naturally occurring elements. Sixty-two percent oxygen, twenty-two percent silicon, six point five percent aluminum, and less than ten percent iron, sodium, potassium, magnesium, and calcium. It took half of Earth's history before one-celled animals evolved."

He is now no more than a shadow. He tries to grip my arm again, but his hand goes right through. "Joss!" he says, his voice raspy and urgent. "I've seen amazing things here. Creatures from environments totally unlike Earth's in almost every way. But they all fight for life, they fight to *be*. The Wipporsims on Angus Beta have barely any gravity to hold them in place. But what good is it to graze the treetops if no one is able to sing about it?"

I want to comfort him. I want to tell him I'll do my best.

With his last breaths, he says, "What humans have achieved in such a short time—our courage, our capacity for love, for joy, for knowledge—you can't let that go. We've taken metals from the ground, forged them into spaceships, and sent them to every planet in our solar system. We are worth saving."

I nod and reach for him, knowing it won't do any good.

He is only a wisp as he gives me a final salute. "When you set out on your journey to Ithaka, pray that the road is long, full of adventure, full of discovery...."

His voice fades into nothing. I watch the spot where he had stood, afraid to turn around and face Annika. The sound of the metal chair hitting the floor leaves me no choice. I turn to find Annika standing beside the toppled chair, tears streaming silently down her face. The notebook and pen lay at her feet.

With a shaky hand, she reaches into her dress pocket and pulls out the white ski cap she wore when she first arrived in The Realms. Still crying, she sticks it on her head, then pulls it down as far as it will go, covering her hair, her eyes, and most of her ears.

For some reason, the image of her vision board flashes before me. I wonder if she's thinking about how much of that stuff might not come true.

She turns to face me, although I don't know how she can see through her hat. "Joss?" she asks, her voice full of sadness.

I step toward her. "I'm here."

She reaches out for my hand. "I want to go home."

The present is the only thing that has no end.
                                                   —Erwin Schrödinger, physicist

16

We run, leaving the Afterlives far behind. We run past the statues of creatures from planets all over the universe. We run past PTB headquarters, now in the shape of a giant ear of corn. We run under a sky the color of nothing. I can't take Annika to her real home, but I can bring her as close as possible. And if I know Aunt Rae, she's already worried about her new houseguest and getting antsy to feed her.

Annika finally stops to rest, panting and gasping. She's still wet from Ty's drenching back in the Afterlives, so I'm not too worried. And the running seems to have dried up her tears. I wait until she catches her breath to ask her the question that's been on my mind since we made our hasty good-byes to Ty.

"Um, Annika?" I begin. "Don't take this the wrong way . . ."

"That's never a good way to start a conversation," she

warns, sitting down on a curb. She yanks off her ski cap and shoves it into her pocket.

All sorts of comments about how funny her hair looks right now fly through my mind, but I force myself to leave them unsaid. Instead, I say, "Well, I just wanted to ask you . . . on Earth, humans live such a short time. If the history of the universe were compressed into one day, humans would have arrived like, one second till midnight."

"And your point is?"

"Well, your lives are over in a blink of an eye, in the scheme of things. And it's not just you guys, most species in the universe are like that. I mean, sure, there are some who have figured out a better way to repair their cells and live a long time, but I guess what I'm wondering is . . ."

"Just spit it out, Joss," she says, sounding tired. "You're not going to offend me."

"Okay. My question is, if you knew you were going to the Afterlives, would it make losing people hurt less?"

Annika doesn't answer at first. I hope I haven't upset her by pointing out her ridiculously short life span. But seriously, it's barely enough time to improve your bowling score by more than a point or two.

She stands up and we start walking. A block away from Kal's house, she finally says, "It would probably make it easier to know that a part of your loved ones gets to live on, yes. But somehow it would take away from the actual living we're supposed to be doing. And what if someone didn't have any days they wanted to relive? Ty wouldn't tell us what the other alternative is. What made you ask that?"

"It was a thought I had when we were leaving. Like maybe people from the planets can't know about The Realms because of the Afterlives. What if that's why any planet that spots us gets destroyed?"

"You mean, not that whole 'against the laws of physics' thing you keep saying?"

Even as I nod, though, I'm reconsidering it. Why kill off a planet to protect it from knowing what happens to them after they die? Then they'd all know when they wound up here. Doesn't make sense, even for the PTB, who often don't make sense to anyone but themselves.

"Seems pretty extreme," she says.

"Yeah, I guess you're right."

"If you don't believe what your father told you, why don't you just ask him for the truth? Isn't he like, the grand pooh-bah, or the great and powerful Oz, or something?"

"Okay, I don't know who those people are, but if you're trying to say Supreme Overlord of the Universe, then yes, he is. And I tried talking to him, but he was practicing his golf swing and wouldn't let me in."

She stops to peer closely at my face, probably to see if I'm joking. Then her mouth quivers at the corners and she smiles again for the first time since she told Carl Sagan she named her cat after him. She jabs me on the arm and says, "Man, your family is not an easy bunch."

"Wait'll you meet the rest of them."

She jabs me again. "Are you inviting me home, Joss Whatever-your-last-name-is? Guess I'm growing on you, huh?"

"Yeah, like mold."

"Hey, don't go dissing mold. Didn't Carl Sagan say mold was responsible for making the oxygen that allowed more advanced life on Earth?"

I shake my head. "I think that was algae. I could be wrong, though."

She sighs. "We're probably not the best people for this project."

"Ya think?"

"What *is* your last name, anyway?"

"I don't have one," I reply. "No need in The Realms. Everyone knows me. I'm Joss, the seventh son."

"But what about all the other kids named Joss? Without, you know, whatever number son they are."

"Others? Why would there be another Joss?" Sometimes Annika has very strange ideas.

We turn the last corner, and I'm relieved to see I'll no longer be squeezing through Lincoln's nostril. I still have scratches on my arms from the rough stone.

Annika stops short. "Is Aunt Rae's house a pie now, or have I gone batty from lack of air?"

"It's a pie."

"That's a relief."

Aunt Rae runs out and meets us as we start up the path.

She's holding what looks like a bunch of leaves and twigs. She scrunches up her nose when she sees Annika. "What happened to your hair, young lady?"

"What's wrong with it?" Annika asks, trying to smooth down the result of wet hair meeting a wool ski cap.

Aunt Rae just shakes her head. "Why don't I get my scissors? A little trim might take some of the fluff right out."

Annika smooths faster. "Um, didn't you cut Joss's hair recently?"

"I certainly did," she says, leaning forward to rumple my hair affectionately.

"Then I think I'll pass. Thanks, though."

"Hey!" I say, smoothing down my own hair now. I shouldn't have told Annika about Aunt Rae cutting my hair. That's it, tonight I'm growing it out.

"Well, this will cover the messy bits," Aunt Rae says, and places what looks like a hat made of leaves on Annika's head. I look closer. It IS a hat made of leaves. Held together by thin twigs, the hat has leaves that tumble over her ears in various shades of green and black. We don't grow plants here, and they are very rare. The few we have were brought back by OnWorlders and always become treasured possessions.

"What is it for?" Annika asks, touching it cautiously.

"It's so you don't have to be wet all the time," Aunt Rae explains. "I traded two of my famous cherry pies to my neighbor down the street in exchange for the branch. He's bragged about owning this plant for the last billion or so years. I think he's grown tired of looking at it, since, honestly, it doesn't do much. He was happy to trade. I twisted the branches into the round shape so hopefully it will stay. As long as you wear it, it will give off all the oxygen you need."

"I have to sleep with this thing?"

"Just rest it next to your head on the pillow, and you'll be fine."

Annika turns her head slowly from side to side and asks me, "How do I look?"

I pause. I don't have much experience with girls, but I'm pretty sure you never answer that question truthfully if the answer is anything along the lines of *weird, strange, odd,* or *like a tree.* I settle on something harmless. "Um, you look fine."

"Fine? That's it? That's all you can say?"

I look to Aunt Rae for help. She says, "You look lovely, Annika."

"Right," I chime in. "That's the word. Lovely."

She rolls her eyes at me and storms into the house.

Girls!

I only have to follow my nose to the kitchen to see I was right about Aunt Rae cooking. The kitchen table is laid out with enough food to feed the whole block for a year. Our food isn't like the food on any of the terrestrial planets. It's more blobby and squishy and bland. Everything except for the pies, and the occasional special treat that someone replicates from a recipe an OnWorlder brings back. Still, Aunt Rae has done an amazing job of making everything look very appealing.

"Who's going to eat all this food?" I ask.

Aunt Rae grabs a pitcher of lemonade from the counter and brings it to the table. "I don't know how much a human needs to eat, so I figured better too much than too little."

Annika runs in, steadying her leaf hat with one hand. "Did someone say *food*?"

I point to the table. "Sit. Eat. Sleep. I have to go home for a little while, but I'll come back for you and we'll plan our next move."

Aunt Rae walks me back to the door as Annika dives into a piece of cherry pie with gusto. I would have picked the pie first, too. With her mouth full, she calls out, "Don't start re-creating the solar system without me!"

"I don't think you need to worry about that," I call back. I can't help but glance at Kal's drum set as we pass by. I haven't heard his drumbeats since we were in the first simulation. I get a pang of fear that maybe that was my last chance.

Aunt Rae sees me looking and puts her hand on my shoulder. "Don't worry, he'll be okay."

I nod, not at all sure she's right. I'm about to thank her for watching over Annika again, when I suddenly realize what she said. And she must have heard Annika's comment about the solar system! We're not supposed to be talking about it in front of Aunt Rae! This is what happens when there are too many secrets. You lose track! What does she know? And how does she know it?

"Um, what do you mean?" I ask nervously. "I'm sure he's having fun OnWorld somewhere with his parents." I have to look away when I say that last part.

"I'm certain you're right," she says, opening the door for me. As she closes it behind me, she says, "You can do more than you think you can."

"What do you—"

But the door shuts behind me before I can ask anything else.

Women!

*You've got to jump off cliffs all the time and build
your wings on the way down.*

—**Ray Bradbury, writer**

17

I'm about to knock on Aunt Rae's door for more of
an explanation, when a voice behind me shouts, "It's
about time you're alone!"

I whirl around. "Kal?"

"Head over to the street and I'll meet you there," he says.
His voice sounds very clear this time. Hardly muffled at all.

I run down the path to the street. I look both ways to
make sure we're alone. Two young boys are kicking a ball
down the block but they don't even glance my way. "Kal,
are you here?"

"I'm here," he says, hurriedly. "Who's the chick?"

"The chick?"

"That's human-speak for girl."

"Oh, the girl! That's Annika. She's the one who saw
Aunt Rae baking the pie!"

"For real?" Kal says. "What's she doing there?"

"She's, er, staying in your room for now. Aunt Rae's watching over her."

"No, I mean, why is she there in The Realms?"

The two boys have stopped playing catch and are watching me now. "Is there somewhere else we can talk?" I ask.

"Just hold up your holoscreen like you're talking into it."

"Oh! Good idea." I fumble in my pocket and pull out the little-used device. Pretending to speak into it, I say, "All I know is that she showed up right when you left. She's going to help me rebuild the solar system and get Earth back. And you and your parents along with it." I don't add the word *hopefully*, although I'm thinking it. "Where are you, anyway? How are you talking to me?"

"You wouldn't believe it. This other universe is totally bizarre and freaky beyond measure. I'm using gravitons to transmit my voice."

"Gravitons? How can you do that?"

"It isn't easy, I'll tell you that. They're the only things that can travel between us. My dad figured it out. It's like . . . wait, what? Mom? Wait! I'm talking to Joss! I didn't get to tell him yet, I was jus—"

"Kal? Are you there?"

A woman's voice answers instead. "Joss? Can you hear me?"

It's Kal's mom! "Yes! I can hear you! We're trying to get you back! We have a plan. Well, sort of a plan!"

"Joss, you have to listen." Her voice is urgent. "The PTB

know what they're doing. If Earth had to be taken out of time, you need to leave it there."

Figures Kal's mom would feel that way. She works for the PTB and is very loyal. But I'm not going to let her sacrifice herself and my best friend. Not when I can do something about it.

"Joss? Do you hear me? You must—"

I wait for her to finish, but she doesn't. I must what? "Hello?" I call out into the air. "Are you still there?" The two little boys are giggling behind me. I've forgotten I'm supposed to be talking into my holoscreen.

No one answers. "All right, then," I say, directing my voice toward my screen. "Thanks for the, uh, visit."

I run all the way home, and by the time I get there, I have a plan. Or the beginnings of one, anyway. I stand in front of the face reader. I expect to see the rest of my family's pictures up on the screens, since anyone who misses Family Picture Day has to deal with the wrath of Mom, and that's not pretty. But only one other face shows up—Ash's. Fortunately, Ash is just the person I need to see to put the plan into action.

"Hello?" I call out.

"Up here," he shouts from the second floor.

I find Ash at his desk, hunched over a book thicker than his arm. Even though we don't sleep much, we each have our own bedrooms where we can go to be alone. It seems like a long time since I've been alone in mine, just playing, or doing homework. Which reminds me that I never wrote my essay. Hopefully my teacher will decide that saving a solar system is more important.

"Hey," I say, plopping down on his bed.

"Hey," he replies, turning the page of his large book.

"Where is everyone? Isn't it picture day?"

He nods, not looking up. "Rescheduled."

"Really?" That almost never happens. With time being so flexible in The Realms, there's rarely a need to change anything around.

"Apparently Dad had some important meeting he couldn't miss. After that, everyone else just left."

"That's too bad," I say, relieved. Picture day is the worst. "Ash, can I ask you something?"

He doesn't reply. I take that as an invitation to continue. I dig in my pocket and pull out one of the confidentiality agreements, which I place on his open book.

"What's this?"

"Just read."

When he gets to the part about cleaning my room for the next millennia, he tosses it aside. "What's this all about, Joss? I'm sorry, but I've got a lot of work to do."

Ash has a very important job, even though, like Bren and me, he's still in school. "I know you're busy creating species in far-flung corners of the universe. I'll be quick."

He closes his book and gives me his full attention. "Is that what you think I do? Create species?"

157

"Isn't it?"

He shakes his head. "I don't actually create anything, or anyone. I just monitor things. I compare the rise of a certain species on one planet with another. I look for mutations, and their sources. I also track the cross-pollination of species via interstellar travel. But create species . . . no."

"I'm sorry," I say, somehow feeling the need to apologize. "That's still a really important job with a lot of important-sounding words. All I do is deliver pies."

He tilts his head and studies me. "Fine, I'll sign it. But only because I'm really curious." He hands back the paper and I blurt out my story, the same one I told Ty in the After-lives. Only this time I add the stuff about meeting Annika's grandfather and the astronomer. I end with, "So then he disappeared before he got to tell us what chemicals were in the people. Gluck said I could find out by testing Annika somehow. Can you help me with that?"

"Why don't you just use the data dots? That's where I get a lot of my information from. I'm sure they'll let you borrow them."

"They did. But they're gone now."

"Gone?"

I look down. "I sort of lost the dots." I can't bring myself to say that someone took them.

"Truly? The whole history of the planet is lost?"

I nod.

He shakes his head, but doesn't reprimand me. "All

right, Joss. I'll help you. You've always been a good brother."

That's just like Ash to say. He looks at things very scientifically, without much judgment. Usually it annoys me. Now I could hug him. I won't, though. That would be weird.

"When do you want to do this?" he asks.

"As soon as Annika wakes up. She's at Aunt Rae's."

He shakes his head. "I don't think so."

Before I ask what he means by that, I hear it, too. The *thump thump thump* of her heartbeat. I look out Ash's transparent wall to see Annika and Aunt Rae approaching the house. They look up and see me. Annika waves. "Hey, Joss! Couldn't sleep! Cool house!"

Ash joins me at the window. "What's in her hair? Did she cross-pollinate with a Florapod?"

"No. It helps her breathe." We leave the room and head downstairs. "You probably shouldn't mention it unless you can say something complimentary."

"I won't mention it, then," he says.

Aunt Rae gestures for Annika to enter, then says, "I have to run. Got a big pie order in."

"Should I deliver them?" I ask. I've never missed work before. I hadn't even thought of it, but they must be piling up.

She shakes her head. "We're okay for now. Don't worry."

She gives Annika a quick hug and rushes out.

"You sure you're not tired?" I ask Annika.

She shakes her head. "Must be something in the food. Or the air. Or the lack of air. I don't know, but I'm not."

"Did you have enough to eat?"

She looks a little sheepish. "Honestly, all I could eat was the pie, which was AMAZING. Everything else was really bad. I'm still kinda hungry."

Ash clears his throat.

"Oh, sorry! Annika, this is my brother Ash. He's the third youngest."

"I prefer fifth oldest," Ash says, reaching out to shake Annika's hand.

"Ash is going to help us figure out what kinds of chemicals are in your body. Gluck says if we know that, we can work backward and that will help us rebuild things."

She turns to Ash. "How would it work?"

"Well, first we drain all your blood, collect the marrow from your bones, slice up your brain, and then analyze it all in the lab. That will tell us the proteins, fats, enzymes, phosphates, chemicals, and…"

Our openmouthed stares stop him from going any further.

"What?" Ash asks, looking back and forth between the two of us. "What's wrong?"

"Seriously?" Annika demands.

He sighs dramatically. "Or…we could scrape a few cells from your arm, pull out a piece of hair, and you could spit in a jar."

Annika taps her chin, pretending to think about it. "Let's go with the second one."

Ash shrugs. "Suit yourself. I can't promise it will be as accurate."

Pushing aside the piece of ivy that has slipped in front of her eyes, she says, "I'm willing to take that chance. Now, what's a girl gotta do to get a bagel with cream cheese and Red Hots around here?"

Every atom in your body came from a star that exploded. And the atoms in your left hand probably came from a different star than your right hand.

—Lawrence M. Krauss, physicist

18

For the tenth time during the short walk to the building where he works, Ash warns us not to touch anything when we get inside. Honestly, he thinks we're children! I'm only nodding politely because he's doing us a big favor.

"I'll try my best not to stick my finger in a socket," Annika promises. "It will be hard, but I'll use all my efforts to make sure I don't flip any *off* switches to *on*, and any *on* switches to *off* and cause anything to accidentally explode."

"That's a good start," Ash says, ignoring her sarcasm, or simply not noticing it.

Like most of the other buildings in The Realms, the Hall of Species is dome-shaped. But where most of the others have transparent walls, these are permanently shaded. It is also the second-largest structure after the Afterlives, and like that one, the inside is much, much bigger than the out-side. I haven't been here since a school field trip when I was younger. Kal got lost in the maze of hallways and it took four teachers to track him down. I hope that wherever he is now, he's safe and he knows I'm trying to help him.

Ash takes out a long key with lots of ridges and nubs. He inserts the key into the lock outside the main door and does some kind of elaborate routine of turning it back and forth in different directions before we hear the click.

I follow Annika into the building, but only get a few feet before I bump right into her. "Ugh!" I rub my nose.

"Sorry," she says absently.

"Is this the wrong kind of light again?" I ask. "Can you see?"

"I can see," she says. "Boy, can I see!" She turns in circles, looking in every direction with wide eyes and an open jaw.

Okay, so the place is pretty cool. Every few feet a holoscreen projects a life-size image of the most advanced species from each terrestrial planet. They revolve slowly, so we can see every angle of their bodies. The variety is astounding, and there is no rhyme or reason in terms of how they are organized, or at least none that I can see. Tiny microbes are next to giant multilimbed creatures, many with scales to protect themselves from the power of their sun. Most of the statues spread around The Realms are based on these projections.

"Where's the human?" Annika asks, unable to tear her eyes away from a golden creature with three legs, four arms, and a mouth wider than Annika's whole head.

Ash gives a little snort. "Humans have been around for only two hundred thousand years, your time. We're still cataloging species two, three million years back. We're a bit understaffed here." Then he brightens. "Hey, we can use *you* as our sample! That will really help us out! Between you and me, I figured we'd have to cross Earth off our list since the reports are gone and, well, Earth is, too."

Annika backs away slowly. "Will it hurt? A few minutes ago you were willing to slice up my brain."

He holds up his hands. "Won't feel a thing, I promise. And just think, you'd be immortalized in The Realms forever." He spreads his arms wide as though to say, *Look around! All this could be yours!*

Annika shrugs. "Sure, why not."

Ash smiles. "Excellent! I haven't had a live specimen to test since . . . well, ever!"

Something occurs to me. "Hey, Ash, do you know why Kal's parents would have wanted the records on humans? Gluck told me they asked for them for some big project they were doing."

He nods. "Kal's mother came herself. Took me a while to find it since, like I said, that data is pretty far down the list."

"She came herself? That's strange. Kal didn't mention his mother was back for a visit."

"She was in a big hurry," Ash replies, lifting a set of keys from a hook on the wall. "She just kept saying it was urgent, but didn't tell me why she needed it. Got me all flustered. Almost gave her the specs for Homins instead of Humans. Pretty different." He chuckles. I can't help chuckling, too, not because Homins are so funny—even though they are—but because it's rare to see anything other than Ash's serious side anymore.

"What's a *Homin*?" Annika asks.

Ash leads us a few yards away and points to one of the holograms. The tiny yellow-and-blue-striped creature is an almost perfectly round ball of fur, except for the two protrusions with big round eyes at the ends. The eyeballs dance inside them to a beat only they can hear. The creature's nose and mouth are tiny, barely visible among all the fur.

Annika eyes it warily. "You pick the most evolved creature on each planet and that's all you could come up with?"

"Press the button," Ash says, pointing to a red circle on the podium below the Homin.

As soon as she does, a deep rumbling voice comes out, reciting what sounds like a mathematical equation. It goes fast, but I catch something like, take forty-two to the twentieth power, multiply by pi cubed, divide something, add something else, and then do a whole bunch of other things I have no hope of understanding.

Ash smiles. "That's the formula for the universe. Only a

few thousand out of the millions of intelligent species in the universe have ever figured it out. Never judge a creature by its size. Or its weird eyes. Or its—"

"Got it," Annika says, holding up her hands. "No judgment."

Ash leads us away, sorting through his large key ring. Annika walks close to me and whispers, "Note how I didn't mention your brother's overly large head. Looks like a bowling ball, that thing!"

I giggle. It may not be manly, but that's what came out. Ash, if he heard, ignores both of us. We follow him through the seemingly never-ending display of the universe's creatures. I give wide berth to the slender Niffum. Even though he's obviously not real, those penetrating eyes and long fingers freak me out. Eventually we reach a wall with a long table against it. The table is dotted with various items from different planets, all with labels in front of them. I recognize a lot of the plant life from learning about them in school, and a lot of the food items, too. Beside me, Annika's belly rumbles.

"Those look really good," she says, pointing to a plate piled high with what look like hot buttered rolls but are actually fermented telimide beans from a planet whose main source of liquid is methane.

"You don't want to try that," Ash says, gently pushing Annika's hand away.

"Why not? I'm really hungry."

"Okay," he says. "Feel free, then."

"Really? Thanks!" Annika reaches for one again.

"No problem," he replies. "So long as you don't mind your stomach exploding as soon as the first bite reaches it. You probably won't feel it, though, since your tongue would have swelled to four hundred times its normal size, causing your head to explode first."

Annika pulls back her hand and sighs. "You could have just said no."

"Just wanted to give you the choice," Ash says. He leads us past the table. "Okay, we're at the lab now. What aren't you supposed to do?"

"Touch anything," we recite in unison.

"Exactly."

I look around us for the lab, but the only door anywhere is a white one marked CLOSET. Ash takes a key from the chain and slips it in the keyhole. The door swings open to reveal a small laboratory. I spot all the high-tech equipment OnWorlders have brought back over the years, some attached to the walls, but most piled up on the floor. Kal would go crazy in here.

Why are all the cool places behind doors marked CLOSET?

"Come on in," Ash says, blowing away the dust clinging to the door. I watch as the dust ball floats slowly to the floor. You almost never see dust in The Realms, since our skin rarely flakes. That only shows how long this room has sat unused.

"This is your lab?" I ask. "It doesn't look like anyone has ever used it."

"They haven't," he replies, moving some boxes out of the way so we can come in. "We've never had anyone to analyze until now." He rubs his hands together and beams at Annika.

She frowns. "Promise no brain slicing."

"You won't feel a thing, scout's honor."

I don't know what a scout is, but it seems to do the trick.

"Okay," Annika says. "Let's get this show on the road, then. We've got a planet to rebuild."

Ash sets to work attaching different pieces of equipment to each other, pouring vials of liquid into various beakers, and generally making the small room feel even smaller. He sets his holoscreen up on the table beside him and says, "All right, take off your shoes and we'll begin."

Annika wrenches off her boots and stands awkwardly in the center of the room. She looks shorter and, for some reason, more vulnerable than I've seen her. Even when she was crying in the Afterlives.

Ash leans toward his screen. "Species: Human. Earth. Orion Arm, Milky Way, Virgo Supercluster. Gender: Female. Name: Annika." He glances up at Annika, who says, "Klutzman." He repeats it. "Annika Klutzman. Looks to be about twelve years of age."

"Almost thirteen!" Annika interjects.

Ash gives her a cursory glance, then turns back to his screen. "Typical human," he dictates. "Not extraordinary in any way."

"Hey!" she says. "That's not true! I'm double-jointed, see?" She clasps her hands behind her back, then brings her arms over her head without her hands pulling apart.

"Not all humans can do that?" Ash asks, interested.

She shakes her head proudly.

"And does that improve your life in any way? Give you an advantage over the rest of your species?"

"Not that I know of," Annika admits, letting her hands drift apart.

"Moving on," Ash says, holding out an empty jar. "Spit in here, please."

She moves her tongue around her teeth, then spits a glob of saliva into the cup. He pours it into the top of a square metallic box that starts humming and beeping.

"Hand," he says. She holds out her hand. He takes what looks like a tiny spoon and gently scrapes it over her palm.

She giggles. "That tickles."

He takes the spoon and pours whatever invisible cells he got into the machine on top of the saliva.

"Now, while that's analyzing, let me just—" He stops talking and, quick as a flash, yanks out a few pieces of hair from Annika's head without even jostling the hat of leaves.

"OW!" she cries, rubbing the spot vigorously. "You could have warned me!" Small pieces of ivy fly from her head.

"Sorry," Ash says, not sounding it. "Needed to get the root intact."

She grumbles and keeps rubbing while he drops the hairs into a long, yellow tube and goes to check the readout from the spit.

"Hmm," he murmurs, holding up the narrow piece of paper that came out of the end of the machine. "Have you recently swum in the tide pools of Shalla in the Pegasus Dwarf Galaxy?"

"Yes, actually," she replies. "Right after I went fishing on Venus."

Ash furrows his brows. "There's no water on Venus. It's much too hot. How could you go fishing?"

She looks to me for help.

"Annika was just kidding," I explain. "She hasn't been off of Earth. Until now, of course."

"Right, right," he says. "I forgot how primitive humanity is."

"There's that word again," she says. "Can I put my shoes back on?"

He nods absently and returns to analyzing his data. "I'll be right back," he says, leaving us alone. Neither of us speaks while Annika laces up her boots, more slowly than necessary.

"Thank you for doing this," I finally say.

"No problem."

Then we're back to no one speaking. The room seems even smaller than it did when we first entered.

"Um, thank you, too, Joss," she says. "For, um, well, for

being such a good friend these last few days. Or however long I've been here. I've lost track."

I figure explaining about how time works differently here can wait, so I just say, "No problem. I'm just glad your brain is still in one piece. You seem very attached to it."

She laughs. "Do you even *have* a brain?"

I pretend to be offended and cross my arms. But then I just shrug and say, "Sort of."

Ash returns to find us grinning at each other. Most of my other brothers would have started teasing me. Ash just hands Annika a small plastic bag, tied up at the end with a string.

She holds it up and we both peer at it. The bottom of the bag is filled with tiny grains of material of various colors, which is strange enough. But at the top of the bag swirling smoke mixes with about a hundred tiny bubbles. "What in the world is *this*?" she asks him.

"Isn't it obvious?" he asks. "It's *you*."

Without water it's all just chemistry. Add water and you get biology. —**Felix Franks, chemist**

19

"M*e?*" Annika asks. "How can I be in a plastic bag? I'm not a sandwich! Although I could use a good grilled cheese and tomato right about now."

"Those are samples of the chemicals in your body," Ash explains, beginning to dismantle the lab equipment. "You're made of oxygen, carbon, hydrogen, nitrogen, calcium, and phosphorus atoms, with a smattering of the other elements found in the soil of your planet." He hands her the printout. "Everything in the bag is listed on here, along with the varying amounts. I gave you all I had. The heavier elements are very hard to come by so don't lose it."

She gives the bag a little shake and frowns. "This is all that's inside me? There's not much here."

"No, no," Ash says. "That's much, MUCH more of each element than what's actually inside you. Trillions and trillions times more. Remember, all creatures are mostly empty space. If you squash the atoms of your whole human race together, squeezing out the empty space between the nucleus and the electrons surrounding it, you'd all fit inside a pinky toe."

"*We'd all fit inside a pinky toe?*" she repeats. "What size pinky toe are we talking about? A baby's? Or like, a sumo wrestler's?"

"Sumo wrestlers can still have small toes," I offer. "I've seen it on the view screens."

"Don't feel so bad," Ash says. "Here in The Realms we have so few atoms in our bodies we wouldn't even fit inside a pinky toenail. *Anyone's* pinky toenail."

While Annika stares at her bag, I take the chance to thank Ash. "I owe you one," I tell him.

"Not at all," he says. "You've helped me, too. Which reminds me!" He turns back to Annika. "Ready to be immortalized?"

"Huh?" she asks. "Oh, right. I get to permanently mingle with all of them." She waves her hand vaguely toward the main hall.

Ash adjusts a large gray knob on the wall. "There's not much mingling, I assure you. Now stand in the center of the floor, please."

I scurry out of the way and Annika takes her place in what's approximately the middle of the room. It's hard to tell with all the mess.

He points to the hat Aunt Rae made. "You'll need to take

that off or for billions of years to come young children on field trips will think humans had leaves growing out of their heads."

She hesitates, then places it on the table and fluffs up her hair. "If my eyes roll back in my head, please let me know."

"Will do."

She smiles at me, showing all her teeth, almost like a grimace. I'm not exactly sure why she's smiling like this, but I can hear my mother's voice saying it would be rude not to smile back. She shakes her head in frustration. "Well? Do I?"

"Do you what?"

"Do I have food in my teeth?"

"Oh! No. You're good."

She smooths down her dress and pinches her cheeks. "Okay, ready!"

A flash of light floods the room for an instant, blinding all of us.

"Sorry about that," Ash says, rubbing his eyes, too. "Like I said, I've never had a live subject before. The other people are generated from old data dot footage."

Blinking rapidly, Annika and I make our way through the main hall and outside to the street. "Never a dull moment here in The Realms," she says, tucking her bag of chemicals into her dress pocket.

"Trust me, there are many dull moments. Eons and eons of them."

"Where to now?" she asks.

I think back to what Professor Sagan was saying about the order of things. "Now that we know what's inside you, I don't think we need to start with the supernova anymore. We can tell what kinds of chemicals must be in your sun now. So let's start there. Let's build a sun!"

"Let's do it!" she says. Then adds, "Is it getting warmer out?"

I shake my head. I'm about to tell her the temperature in The Realms never changes when I notice her eyes are becoming glassy. And it's not from the flash of light. "Lie down," I command her. "I'll be right back."

I race inside, darting around the holo figures to the back room. The hat of leaves is right where Annika placed it. I grab it without a word to Ash, who whistles as he manipulates the new holo image of Annika, now projected right where she was standing. My brain (which I *do* have, even if I couldn't readily explain that to Annika earlier) registers that the holoviewer did an excellent job of capturing not just her image, but her personality somehow. I run back out to find Annika panting, but still conscious. She grabs the hat and throws it back on her head.

"I'm really sorry," I tell her. "I feel like I'm not taking very good care of you."

"You are," she insisted, her breathing already becoming steady again. "Now let's go build a sun!"

I shake my head. "I'm taking you back to my house. You need to eat. My mom makes the best grilled cheese and tomato sandwich in all The Realms."

"Really?"

I shake my head. "No. We don't usually get to eat things like that. But I'm sure she'll figure it out."

Annika spends the whole walk talking about her family and her cat and her friends and school. I spend the whole walk listening. Being an almost-teenager on Earth sounds exhausting. I now know that her favorite subject in school is Language Arts because they get to pick whatever book they want to read. Her least favorite is History because she "can't keep all the dead dudes straight." I know her brother wiggles his butt when he gets in trouble so everyone will laugh and forget what he did wrong. And I know that her mother can make her own hair into a perfect French braid with her eyes closed.

I even know that her friend Rachel has a crush on a pop star whose name is the same word as a foot fungus that is rapidly spreading through the Cartwheel Galaxy. Annika laughs when I tell her that. "I can't wait to tell Rachel." Then she frowns. "If I ever get the chance."

"So this is Annika!" my mother exclaims, throwing her arms around Annika even before we're halfway in the door. Then she steps back in delighted surprise. "Why, she's so solid!"

I nod.

"Yup," Annika says. "I've heard that."

I glance up at the screen to see who's home. Besides Mom, it's just Bren. I clock in and my face joins his.

"Neat!" Annika says.

"Mom, will you feed Annika while I talk to Bren?"

"Of course!" Mom says, putting an arm around Annika. "I'm sure us girls will find lots to talk about."

Maybe this wasn't such a good idea. I pause, but Mom is already guiding Annika down the hall and pointing at the holographs. Hopefully she'll skip past the more embarrassing ones.

I feel my pocket for another confidentiality agreement for Bren. Not that there's anything I want his help with, but I need to tell him what's been going on. It feels weird keeping it from him, more than anyone. I call his name, but he doesn't answer. That's not unusual, since he often has headphones on. I check his room. Since Bren's job involves testing all the new technologies from the inhabited planets, he spends a lot of time in his room with his friends. I'm always invited to join, but usually I'm hanging out at Kal's house, or down at Thunder Lanes. I linger in the doorway and wonder if I'll spend more time here now. Then I shake the thought out of my head. I'm going to bring Kal back. No room for doubt.

I'm about to turn away when I notice a large lump under Bren's bedcovers. Since we spend so little time in bed, the covers are almost always flat, the bed tightly made. Maybe it's a new video game he doesn't want me to see. Nearly every civilization that makes it as far as making moving pictures quickly follows it up with video games. I can't imagine why Bren would hide a new one, though. Sure, he knows I'm jealous of his job, but who wouldn't be?

We have a strict rule in the house to respect each other's

privacy. I haven't snooped in any of my brothers' rooms in thousands of years. I don't want to end that streak now, over some video game.

But if he took the time to hide it, it must be really cool.

I rush over to the bed and pull back the covers before I change my mind. I stare down at the last thing I'd expected to see.

My box of data dots.

And the worst part? It's empty.

The Sun, with all the planets revolving around it, and depending on it, can still ripen a bunch of grapes as though it had nothing else in the Universe to do. —Galileo, mathematician

20

Our house is not that big. Okay, it's sort of big. Not Afterlives big, or Hall of Species big, though. I should be able to find one teenage boy. There aren't that many places to hide. I've checked in all the closets, under the beds, in the art room, the music room, the entertaining room, the laundry room. I even looked in the storage area beneath the stairs where Bren and I used to hide when we were younger (okay, sometimes we still do). But no sign of him. Either he's found a new, really good hiding spot, or he left and forgot to clock out, which means he'll feel Mom's wrath. She considers leaving without clocking out as bad as not coming home in the first place.

By the time I get back down to the kitchen, my anger has turned to disappointment and confusion. Was Bren really trying to ruin the project? Is he jealous that I'm finally doing something more important than delivering pies? Or was he just playing a joke and doesn't understand the importance of why I needed that data? I'll need to find him to ask him.

My mother and Annika are sitting at the table, hunched over some book. Annika points and says, "That's him?" Mom nods and they both burst out laughing. I get a sinking feeling.

"That's not my..." But I see that it is. Mom is showing Annika my sixth-grade graduation holograph. Doing something like that should be illegal! Sixth-grade pictures in general should be illegal! Capturing that awkward gawky phase is just not fair, and I was stuck in it for soooo long. Longer than any of my classmates, as I recall. I reach over and snatch the book away.

"Aw, don't be mad," Annika says, reaching for her last bite of sandwich. "I think you look adorable. And your ears grew to match your head, so it's all good."

I force myself to calm down, because I don't want to yell at my mother for embarrassing me. I would only sound like a brat and get more embarrassed. So I just shove the book into a kitchen drawer and shut it firmly. "Mom," I say, trying to keep my voice steady, "have you seen Bren? His picture is on the screen but I can't find him."

She shakes her head. "I haven't seen him. Annika and I have been having a lovely conversation, though. She tells me you're planning to rebuild her planet?" She says this lightly, almost breezily, like she's just making conversation. But I can hear the undercurrent of surprise and an edge of accusation.

I glare at Annika, who goes on chewing, oblivious to the fact that she just spilled the biggest secret I've ever had. Do I dare ask my mom to sign one of the confidentiality agreements? I don't have the nerve. So I tell her the story, even about Kal disappearing and his parents being on Earth. The only part I leave out is about Kal contacting me from another universe. I'm afraid to risk him or his parents getting into some kind of trouble and maybe being stuck there if I say the wrong thing, or tell the wrong person. The idea of there even *being* other universes is so huge that I can't risk it. I also don't tell her about finding the empty box of stolen data dots in Bren's room. That's between him and me.

I finish up by making it clear that I had repeatedly told Gluck I wasn't the best person for the job, that I'm a pie deliverer and not a solar-system builder, and that I have no idea how I'm actually supposed to make this happen, but that I'm going to finish as best I can.

"And I'm helping," Annika chimes in, adjusting her leaves so they're not covering her eyes. "I'm in a bag!"

My mother tilts her head at that comment, then shakes it and turns back to me. "C'mere," she says, opening up her arms wide.

I'm surprised. Mom is not usually the warm, huggy type. But I move forward into her arms, feeling a little awkward in front of Annika. Still, it would be more awkward to refuse.

My mother's arms are strong and I feel myself relax. I close my eyes and the darkness is comforting. "Joss." Her voice is a whisper, and I can tell it's in an audio range Annika can't hear. "Joss," she repeats. "I'll keep your secret, but of course I can't help you, since I would never go against what your father ordered."

"I would never ask you to," I reply in the same low tone.

"But I will tell you one thing: You do more than deliver the pies."

I pull away. "What do you mean?" I ask, in my regular voice.

Mom glances at Annika, then seems to decide she can be trusted. "You do more," she says, emphasizing each word, "than deliver the pies."

"I know," I reply. "I go to school, too. Well, I may have missed a few days...."

"That's not what I meant," she says. But she abruptly stands up instead and busies herself clearing the table from Annika's lunch. Annika jumps up to help and the two of them giggle again at the sink. I watch them and think for the first time, ever, that maybe my mother might have wanted a girl instead of the seven boys she wound up with.

"Are you okay?" Annika asks as she watches me put my face in front of the reader. Just because Bren didn't follow the rules doesn't mean I'm about to break them.

I nod. "Let's just go." I don't want to get into all the emotions I'm feeling. It's too much, and I need to focus.

Annika follows me out, swinging the bag of snacks my mom packed her. "Where are we going?"

"To find my brother Laz. He's the middle child— number four—and can be a pain. But he'll know how to build a sun."

"I have no idea how to build a sun," Laz says when we find him on the hillside behind PTB headquarters (which is currently in the shape of a three-legged toad). He is sipping a cold drink and lounging on a beach chair. If I thought my job was easy, Laz's is almost ridiculously simple. All he does is lie on his chair in front of a giant view screen of an ocean. We don't have real oceans in The Realms, obviously, but this helps Laz to imagine a horizon like on the planets. Every once in a while Laz waves a stick in the air and the sun on the view screen begins to descend. He flicks a button on his chair and the scene changes to another beach, this one with two suns in the sky. Personally, I think they stuck him with this job to keep him out of trouble. Working on his own like this means he can't argue with his coworkers.

"What do you mean you can't make a sun?" I ask. "We know all the ingredients, we just need to know how to put it all together. Isn't it your job to control sunrises and sunsets?"

He shrugs. "I don't really control them, more like

manage them. Or, technically, *watch* them, I suppose." He takes another long sip of his drink.

I push the confidentiality agreement I had been holding back into my pocket. I don't even need to waste this one on him.

"Joss, wait," Laz says, as we turn to go. "I may not know how to make a sun, but when I was training for my job—"

Annika interrupts. "You have to train to sit on a chair and wave a stick at a screen?"

"Okay, fine," Laz snaps. "While I was doing my very quick, blink-and-you-miss-it training for this job, I saw a really old part of The Realms. Like back when the universe was new and stars and planets were just being built. I bet if you go there you'll find what you need."

"Thanks, Laz," I say, feeling a little guilty that I was so quick to dismiss him. "Do you want to know why we need to build a sun?"

"Nah," he says, leaning back in his chair. "I figure you've got your reasons."

Laz is an odd one. Either he's all fired up about something, or he can't be bothered to act even remotely interested.

He does give us the directions, though, ending with, "You'll know it when you see it." Before we leave, he gives Annika a long look. "Bum luck about your planet there. Sorry to hear of it."

"Um, thanks," she says. "It's been ... difficult."

He nods sympathetically, then turns his attention back to his view screen and waves his stick at it.

"You have a strange family," Annika comments as we head back the way we came.

"Don't I know it," I reply, looking up at PTB headquarters. I'm not sure which office is my father's now. The toad's head? His rump? Dad's definitely been avoiding me. Or at least it feels that way.

When we get to the other side of the building, I stop short. The statues of Kal's parents have been completed! There have been a few alterations since the blueprint I saw. For one, Kal's mother is now wearing pants, which would certainly please her, and Kal's father is holding a hot dog in one hand and a cup of lemonade in the other. Is he supposed to be at a summer barbecue? Maybe Aunt Rae saw these statues and that's why she suspected something earlier. Soon everyone will know. I want to throw a blanket over the statues, cover them up somehow, buy some time to get them back before the grieving sets in.

"Hey," Annika says, looking the statues up and down. "I know those guys!"

I shake my head. "No you don't. Those are Kal's parents. They just look more human than most of us because their job was to blend in on Earth."

"No," she insists. "I really do know them. That's Rose and Marvin Sheinblatt from down the street. Marvin and my dad used to go fishing and stargazing together."

I know she's mistaken, because OnWorlders are never allowed to make close friends. But the last thing I want to do right now is argue, and a small crowd has started to gather around us. I take Annika's elbow and steer her quickly away to avoid them.

We don't get too far when I begin to hear the drumbeats. They start softly, then grow stronger and more insistent. I stop and call out Kal's name.

Annika puts her hand on my arm, alarmed. "Joss, are you all right? What are you doing? No one is here."

"Do you hear it?" I ask. "The drumbeats? Do you hear them?"

She shakes her head.

The drumming has become almost frantic now. I excuse myself and run a few yards away. Maybe he can only talk to me in private. But as quickly as it began, the drumming cuts off. Ice trickles down my back. I have a feeling Kal and his parents aren't safe there much longer. How quickly can an entire universe collapse? Or maybe whoever the Supreme Overlord is (if there is one) has them locked up deep underground somewhere!

I rejoin Annika and explain to her about Kal and the drums and how frustrating it is not to be able to reach him.

"Another universe?" she asks. "I'm still trying to wrap my head around this one! What's the other one like?"

"I don't know," I tell her honestly. "But from what we learned in school, probably nothing like this one. I think it's really unstable. Like the laws of physics aren't working there."

"Oh. That doesn't sound good. I'm sorry."

She sounds so sincerely sorry that I feel the need to

change the subject. "Hey, so I found the empty box that those data dots were in. The ones that were stolen."

I hadn't meant to tell her that. I guess she's pretty easy to talk to. For a girl.

"You *did*? Where?"

"My brother Bren took them." I cringe a little as I say the words out loud. It still stings.

"Bren? Isn't he your favorite brother? I thought you guys were really close."

I nod. "I thought so, too."

We walk in silence for a while. I'm half-wishing Annika would continue her tales of teenage girl angst, so I wouldn't have to think about how everything I thought might be wrong. But she stays uncharacteristically quiet. I've never been to the part of The Realms that Laz described, and after walking for what feels like a very long time, I'm beginning to wonder if he sent us way out here as a gag. He's not really a joke-playing kind of guy, though—that's more Bren's and Grayden's territories. And mine, I guess.

"Are you sure this is right?" Annika asks, as though reading my mind. She, too, is looking around at the nothingness that surrounds us. We left the buildings and houses and statues behind long ago. Even the view beneath our feet has grown dim, like we're above an area of space almost entirely devoid of stars.

"Let's keep going a little farther," I say as we begin to climb a gentle slope. "Laz said we'd know it when we saw it, so . . ." The words dry up in my mouth. Annika gasps and grabs my arm. We both stare, openmouthed, at the scene in front of us. I'm not sure she can see all that I can see, but clearly what she sees is enough to cause her stunned reaction. If there's a word for the complete and total opposite of *nothing*, that's what we're looking at. This is truly something. It's...EVERYTHING.

Trillions and trillions of hydrogen atoms, the most primordial of all of the elements in the universe, are swirling around in a massive cloud as high as I can see. They float and zip and dodge around each other in a graceful and chaotic dance. I can see right into them, in a way I've never been able to before. I can see the single proton inside the nucleus, and inside that, packets of pure energy, the quarks. The single electron forms a blurry cloud, protectively, almost as if to say *Buzz off, this proton's mine, get your own*.

Annika slowly unfurls her fingers from my arm. We both look down to see five deep furrows. They will take a little time to fill back in again. "Sorry," she whispers. "Forgot how squishy, I mean *softish*, you are."

I look up at her face. Funny how foreign it was to me not that long ago, and how familiar it is to me now. I smile and she returns my grin, her eyes glassy and bright and full of confidence in me. Me! I am filled with the same sensation that comes over me when I deliver a pie, a fullness that starts at my feet and goes up the rest of my body.

I turn back to face the roiling, spinning mass of primordial atoms and reach out my hands. I feel the space around me shift, and my palms get warmer. The heaviness settles in my limbs, connecting me to the ground in a way that I've never experienced before.

I allow my palms to move closer together until there is hardly any space between them. I push and squeeze and my whole body gets hotter and hotter and I don't know why I know how to do this, or why I'm not burning up. I can feel the hydrogen atoms trying to avoid each other, spinning and spinning until the pressure becomes too much and they surrender, allowing their nuclei to merge into one blazing-hot core.

And just like that, the sun ignites.

What is it that breathes fire into the equations and makes a universe for them to describe?
—Stephen Hawking, theoretical physicist, cosmologist

21

I move my hands apart, so slowly it's barely noticeable. But each time I do, the heat increases and the baby sun gets bigger. By the time my hands reach my sides, the sun has grown so big, so bright, so hot, that the hydrogen atoms start turning into helium, exactly what needs to happen to keep the sun going. The whole electromagnetic spectrum shoots out in all directions and the force of it knocks me off my feet.

Annika has run far to my right. To my left, I hear the echo of frenzied drumming. How long has it been going on and I hadn't noticed? "I'm coming for you, Kal, hold on!" I say this out loud, not caring how it sounds. It's not like anyone is around to hear besides Annika. I turn to check on her and find her waving her arms and pointing behind her.

A figure appears at the top of the slope. Our surroundings are so incredibly bright that all I can see is a bulky shape with arms and legs.

The shape gets closer, and my eyes widen as I recognize who the wide chest and thick legs belong to. "Thade?"

In an instant he's beside me. "Joss!" he yells, even though I'm inches away. "What are you doing?"

"Why are you yelling?" I yell back, realizing that the new sun is making a lot of noise. Banging and swooshing and churning types of sounds scream from it in all directions. "Did Laz tell you I was here?"

"Yes!" he yells.

Guess I should have given him the confidentiality agreement after all.

"Are you doing that?" Thade shouts, pointing to the ever-growing sun.

I hesitate, then shout, "I think I am!"

"Impressive!" he roars, clasping me on the shoulder.

Thade isn't my father, of course, but he's so much older than I am that he might as well be. His praise makes me stand a little taller. "Um, thanks?" I say, uncertainly. "You're not mad? I thought there might be some consequences to trying to build a solar system inside The Realms."

"Oh, I'm mad. And there will certainly be consequences. But tell me why you're doing this?"

I thrust the agreement into his hand. He glances at it and crumples it up.

"It's too late for this," he says. "The Powers That Be

already know something's going on out here. The shock waves from your new sun can be felt all over The Realms. Does this have to do with the new statue outside PTB headquarters? Of your friend's parents?"

I hesitate again, then nod.

"You're trying to get them back? And Earth, too, I'm guessing?"

The drumming is growing louder, more insistent. I can hear it clearly over the sun now. "Yes," I reply. "The whole solar system."

"What is that?" Thade asks, looking around us. "Is someone playing the drums?"

"You can hear it?" I ask excitedly. "It's Kal! He and his parents are trapped in another universe and—"

Thade holds up his hand. "There *are* no other universes."

"Okay," I shout, "we'll deal with that later. Right now I need your help building planets and getting them in the right places. That's what your job is, right?"

Now he's the one who hesitates. "I don't actually make them. The planets form out of the dust and gas released from the birth of a star. You know that from school. Their orbits are determined by the gravity between the star and the planet, and the speed of the planet when it originally formed. My job is to monitor all that. We can talk about our job descriptions later. You have to focus! You have a sun to control!"

My sun (MY sun!!) has grown so big that I can barely see

around it on any side. Panic sets in. "Thade! I'm still pretty sure I'm the wrong person for this job!"

Thade reaches over and tilts up my chin until his furry brows are level with my eyes. "Joss, you are the *only* person for this job. You still don't understand that, do you?"

"What do you mean?"

"You have one of the most important jobs in the universe. Without you, nothing would exist. Nothing would have gravity, or weight."

I make a choking sound and shake my head. "I deliver pies, that's all."

"No," he says, his voice firm. "You don't just *deliver* the pies."

The memory of Mom saying those same words floats back to me. "I don't?"

He shakes his head. "When you—and only you—carry the pies, they absorb mass like a sponge and increase their weight." He pauses, then chuckles. "Hey, the pie makers should really be making sponge cakes instead of pies." He jabs me in the arm. "Get it? Sponge cakes?"

Now is the time Thade decides to develop a sense of humor?

"Okay, bad joke," he admits, waving it off. "So anyway, the Powers That Be send the pies out into the expanding universe. Once they get where they're going, they provide the gravity that pulls the interstellar gases together. You, little brother, start the stars."

His words seem utterly impossible to believe. But there's that heaviness that I've never been able to explain when I pick up the pies. And I felt it again just now, with the sun, only so much stronger. Does that mean...no, he can't be right. But Thade is never wrong, or at least I've never known him to be.

"How can that be?" I ask. "Why should I be able to do that and not you? Or Dad?"

He smiles. "Because *you* are the seventh son."

"But...but why didn't someone tell me before now?"

He shrugs. "We figured you'd get a big head if you knew how important you were. We had to protect you from your own ego."

I stare at him, dumbfounded. I could have used some of that confidence instead of thinking I didn't have anything to contribute.

"Hey, don't look at me like that. I'm only joking. We knew you'd put it all together someday. Everyone comes into their talents when they're ready, Joss. You're ready now. So keep going! You can do this!"

With Thade's revelation hanging in the air, and the sun expanding before me, I suddenly remember Annika. I whirl around and shout her name.

"Over here!" a thin voice replies. "Behind the hill! In the cave!"

I run over to the lip of the ridge and find her tucked underneath an overhang, barely a cave at all. But it does a good job of protecting her from the activity on the other side of the ridge. "I need the bag from Ash. Do you still have it?"

With a shaking hand, Annika reaches into her pocket. Our hands linger ever so briefly when she passes me the ingredients. "Annika, are you holding up okay? Are you hurt at all?"

"How are you doing this, Joss?" she whispers.

"Somehow I just know what to do," I reply honestly. I don't think I can explain what Thade just told me. Not now, anyway.

"Go on, then," she says, waving me away. "Send me back home."

I squeeze her shoulder as reassuringly as I can and run back to the sun. Getting as close as I dare, I open the bag and throw the contents right into the churning ball of gas. When Thade sees what I've done, he grabs me and hauls me back over the ridge to where Annika is now huddled into a ball.

It doesn't take long for me to realize why he did this. Once the chemicals sink into the center of the sun, chunks of rock and debris begin flying out in all directions, some landing on this side of the hill. My planets are being born! "I have to get back!" I shout, trying to pull away from Thade's grasp. "I'll be careful, I promise. I have to get the planets in the right orbits! I have to get Jupiter in place to protect Earth, I have to form the moon, I—"

But he holds me there. "Patience," he says. "Wait until some of the rocks have stuck together. There's nothing you can do until then."

So we sit. I try to think clearly as the heat from the sun grows stronger and stronger, quicker than I'd have thought possible from how it was growing. What had the professor said comes next? Comets with water need to hit Earth? Where do I find those? And then life. Where do I get amino acids? I nudge Annika.

"Do you still have those two data dots?"

She looks confused, then remembers. "Yes! They..." Her face falls. "They're on my dresser at Aunt Rae's."

A huge explosion drowns out my next thought. It is the single loudest noise I've heard in my life. I instinctively throw myself over Annika, and Thade throws himself over me. We huddle there, in a pile, for what seems like forever. Finally the air stops vibrating with noise and heat and rubble and broken things.

"Um, I think you can get off me now," Annika says, her voice muffled.

Thade lifts off first, then I untangle myself and kneel on the grass beside them. Annika smooths her dress and tries to adjust the leaf hat, which is mostly in tatters now. I know without looking that my sun is gone, along with the baby planets.

"I'm sorry, kid," Thade says, his voice thick. "You gave it your best shot."

Chances are, when we meet intelligent life-forms in outer space, they're going to be descended from predators.　　　　　　**—Michio Kaku, physicist**

22

I'm up on my feet and running back over the ridge. The ground is scorched a deep black. But something else covers the sizzling debris. Something filmy, which bubbles and glides as it spreads. I approach cautiously, and dip my finger into it. Water! Where did water come from all the way out here? Is that what made my sun explode?

A speck of movement in the corner of my eye catches my attention. I whip my head around in time to see a tiny figure disappear into the distance. I run back over the ledge. "Thade! Will you make sure Annika gets back to Kal's house safely? I have to do something."

"Okay, but the Powers That Be will—"

Without giving him a chance to say more, I take off at a run, back in the direction of the central Realms. Every now and again I catch a glimpse of the figure, running faster than should be possible. I concentrate hard, and my legs turn into wheels. I pick up speed as I race forward, trying not to feel every pebble and uneven patch of ground. Bruises are already starting to form, and it takes a lot for our skin to bruise. But I refuse to lose sight of him.

As I approach the populated areas, everything rushes toward me in a blur. I slow down, stumbling to a stop. I shake my wheels into legs again, and hobble around to get the feeling back into them. I'm in a neighborhood not too far from my school. I can hear the kids talking and the occasional burst of laughter. It all seems so *normal*.

I turn all around, but don't see anyone who looks like he'd just been running from an exploding sun. In frustration and exhaustion, I plop down on the ground and lean up against one of the many Grayden-inspired statues. This one is dressed as a winged fairy-like creature with a pointy hat and a wink.

Do I try to remake the sun? I'd have to get all the chemicals from Ash again. No, I can't do that. He said he'd given us all the ones he had. We'd have to start with a supernova, and generate all the elements the normal way. Could I do that? Could I make a sun huge enough that it could go supernova? Did I just lose my last chance to save Kal and get Annika back to her family? My thoughts are swirling so fast it takes a while before I realize I'm being watered, like a plant. I look up to see where the drops are coming from. There, hiding atop the statue, is my brother Bren, slowly losing his grip on the statue's pointy hat.

Our eyes meet. Mine narrow into slits. "Hey, little bro!" he says cheerily. "Some help here?"

I just stare up at him. I should have known. First he takes the data dots, then right when the solar system gets going, he sabotages it.

"Help?" he asks again.

I shake my head.

"C'mon, Joss, don't be that way."

I purse my lips and cross my arms.

He sighs. "Fine." Then he lets go and drops to the ground. Instantly he's up and running.

He's fast. But I'm faster. I tackle him before he can reach the other side of the statue.

"Why, Bren?" I ask, holding down his arms. "Why did you do it?"

A small part of me registers that Thade is sprinting up the street toward us, with Annika on his back. Bren tries to pull away, but I hold him down.

"Kal told me to," he says.

"Kal?" My grip loosens slightly out of surprise and Bren takes the opportunity to wiggle out of my grasp. He doesn't run away, though. "I was right around the corner from his house when I heard his voice coming from nowhere. I thought it was a trick, but he convinced me it wasn't. He told me the box outside his house was his, that he'd left it there by mistake before he went to visit his parents OnWorld somewhere. I was just doing him a favor by holding on to it. Or so I thought. It wasn't until I saw the

199

labels on the data dots that I thought maybe he'd lied to me."

I sit back on my heels, dumbfounded by all this. "That makes no sense. Kal *wants* me to rebuild the solar system. He wants me to get him and his parents back."

Thade and Annika reach my side. "Are you all right?" Annika asks. She looks down at my banged-up legs and gasps. "What happened to you?"

"Wheels," I reply, only half paying attention. My head is spinning from Bren's revelations.

"Rats," she says. "I missed it!"

"Hi, I'm Bren," Bren says, extending his hand to Annika.

She narrows her eyes at him. "You're the one who stole Joss's data dots!"

"I was going to give them back," Bren says. "Eventually."

She still doesn't shake his hand. "We could have rebuilt the solar system twice by now if we'd had those!"

Bren lowers his arm. "That's the point. Kal didn't *want* you to rebuild it. Well, he *does*, but not yet. He thought taking the box would put the project on hold. Then when he realized that you'd made the sun on your own, he sent me to put it out."

I stare at my brother, my second-best friend. What kind of story is he making up? Maybe he really is jealous. Maybe he knew about the seventh-son thing all these years and has now decided to ruin things for me.

"Turns out," Bren continues, "that you can't put out a sun with water. It just made it hotter till it grew and grew and then exploded." He widens his arms. "Boom, like that."

"You're not making any sense," I tell him. "Why wouldn't he want me to rebuild it as soon as possible? He and his parents—"

"You mean the Sheinblatts," Annika interrupts.

I groan. "No, not the Sheinblatts."

Thade breaks in. "Annika! How did you know their OnWorld name?"

I whip my head toward Thade so fast my neck hurts. "What? She's right?"

Annika lifts her chin. "Told you."

Thade stares at Annika with such intensity that she flinches a bit. "Well?" he demands. "How do you know their names? The OnWorlders' code names are closely guarded."

Annika moves slightly closer to me, then says, "Um, they were friends with my parents. I didn't know they had any kids, though. They lived down the street. The husband—Marvin, I mean—used to stargaze with us. He made the best homemade chili on the block. Next to my own father's, of course."

The three of us just stare at her. *Kal's dad made homemade chili?* The men in The Realms really aren't that skilled in the kitchen.

"Was he there with you the night you looked into the scope and found us?" Thade asks.

Annika nods. "He gave my dad a new telescope that

night, so we could look at Mars. It was a gift for my dad's forty-fifth birthday. It was really fancy, like with a computer attached to it and everything, you know, where you put in the coordinates, and then the telescope moves to the right place?"

Her words sink in. My brothers and I exchange a look. I know we're all thinking the same thing. But it's too outrageous. Too unbelievable. Had spending so much time OnWorld made Kal's parents so uncaring about what would happen after someone looked in that telescope?

"Maybe," I begin, my voice shaking, "maybe Kal's dad gave Annika's father his own scope by mistake? The coordinates of Aunt Rae's kitchen would have been in there so he could check on Kal. That makes sense, right?"

Annika shakes her head. "It was definitely not theirs. I saw him take it out of a new box. He set it up for my dad and everything."

"But was he still there when you were looking through it?" Thade asks.

"No," Annika says. "It was really late, and he had to go to the office the next day. I think he worked in insurance or something."

Bren stifles a laugh. An insurance-selling, chili-making version of Kal's dad is just too ridiculous. Then I remember that last data dot, the one Annika was watching in her room. The only way her family would have wound up being recorded was if the OnWorlders had been nearby. Down the block would certainly be close enough. My head feels like it's going to make a bigger boom than the sun did.

"But why?" I ask. "Why would they have wanted Annika to see The Realms? They knew what would happen after. They loved Earth. Why would they want to see it destroyed?"

"The Sheinblatts would never destroy the planet!" Annika insists. "Rose had just planted tomatoes!"

We look at Bren for answers. He shrugs. "Dunno. I just did what Kal asked. Why don't you ask him yourself?"

"How can I do that?" Then I hear it, too. The drumbeats. "Do you hear Kal's voice?" I ask Bren.

He shakes his head. "Not yet. It's been harder for him to make contact lately."

"Make contact from where?" Thade asks. "Where is he hiding?"

"He's in another universe," Bren replies. "Pretty cool, eh?"

"Told you," I can't resist saying to Thade.

"But there are no other—"

"Have any of you looked in a mirror lately?" Kal says, cutting off any further argument on the subject of other universes. His voice seems to come from behind the winged statue. "You guys are a mess!"

We all jump up and start talking to the statue at once. "Where are you, Kal? What's going on? Why did your parents—"

"Let the statue talk!" Annika shouts.

Bren leans toward Annika. "It's not really the statue talking, you know."

"Hey, I've seen some strange things lately," she says, glaring at him. "A talking statue wouldn't surprise me one bit."

I step out of the group. "Kal, please, what's going on? Why did your parents want to destroy Earth by letting Annika see into The Realms? That's pretty much the complete opposite of their job description."

"Hey there, old pal!" Kal says, almost cheerfully. "Been crazy lately, right?"

"Kal!"

"Okay, okay, sorry! They weren't trying to destroy Earth. They were trying to save it. They needed to get everyone out of the way for a while. They didn't have much time, and this was the best solution they could think of. They knew the Powers That Be would pull the planet out of time after Annika spotted The Realms."

"But how did they know that?" I ask. "The PTB could have exploded it instead."

"They have a contact person on the inside," Kal says. "Someone who had promised to help them. The contact also promised to help them restore it. They couldn't reveal too much, though, or risk being pulled from the operation."

I have a feeling I know exactly who their "contact" is, and his name ends in "the Yuck." I guess I'll have to come up with a nicer nickname. Although maybe not, since he kept so much from me. Unless he didn't know it himself.

"Joss," Kal says, "I never thought—and my parents never thought—that it would be you who would have to do this, I swear."

Before I can reply, Annika reaches out and touches the statue's wing. "Kal?"

Bren leans over to her and whispers out of the corner of his mouth, "I told you he's not really in there."

"I know!" she hisses. Clearly she hasn't forgiven him for stealing the films. I'm not so sure I have, either. "Kal," she repeats. "It's Annika. You know, from Earth? I don't understand. Why did your parents need to do this? To get everyone out of the way, like you said?"

Kal doesn't answer immediately, and I feel a rising panic that we've lost him again. Finally, he says, "It's because of the Niffum, Annika-from-Earth. They're on a direct course through the Milky Way. Next stop, your home planet."

At the mention of the Niffum, Thade, Bren, and I stiffen.

Annika looks surprised. "Isn't that the species you're not supposed to turn your back on in the rain?"

I try to say *Yes, or any other time*, but it comes out more like a whimper.

She shakes her head. "Honestly, you're scared of something called a Niffum? Sounds so cute and cuddly. Like a kitten."

It's not. The Niffum from the Cygnus Galaxy are one of the oldest and most advanced civilizations in the universe. Their planet was so well protected from harm that life started very early and thrived longer than any other. But all good things come to an end, and as their star burned out, they began to seek out new homes. They set a course for any planet with the right kind of atmosphere, and they don't even bother to learn if life already exists there. They simply take over the planet, destroying every living thing that isn't compatible with their own biology. Which is mostly everything. I'm sure all of us are thinking about what would happen to the people of Earth if the Niffum showed up.

Well, all of us except for Annika, who breaks the silence by asking, "Does anyone notice this statue looks a lot like Grayden?"

> *The book of nature is written in the language of mathematics.* —Galileo, mathematician

23

"Wake up!" Annika shouts in my ear. "I thought no one slept in The Realms."

"Once a month," I mumble, throwing the pillow over my head. "Just let me sleep a little longer."

"I thought you didn't care about time."

I groan. If she's going to throw everything I've ever said back at me, I'm NEVER going to get any sleep. I toss the pillow off in defeat and sit up. "Fine. I'm awake."

She giggles. "You have bed head. And a long crease on your cheek."

I close my eyes, shake my head, and my hair and cheek puff out nicely. I've been practicing maintaining my appearance better.

"I kind of liked it better the other way," she teases. "Oh well! Get out of bed, we're going to school."

I groan again. Ever since my failed attempt at building a

sun (otherwise known as Bren's Enormous Act of Sabotage and Treachery, or BEAST), Annika hasn't let me miss a day of school. It's been nearly two months (her time) that she's been stuck here, and she's trying to make the best of it. Each day the Niffum get closer to where Earth used to be, and each day we try to pretend we aren't worried about what's going to happen when they get there. Going to school takes both of our minds off it, at least for a little while.

Annika likes to tag along with me, which in the beginning was a bit annoying. She got a lot of attention from the other kids (obviously, being so solid and all) and a lot of sympathy from the teachers (who don't know anything about the real reason her planet was pulled out of time, nor our plans to try again to restore it once the danger has passed). Other than Bren and Thade, no one except Mom and Aunt Rae knows that Kal's parents were behind all this. The fewer people who know, the safer their secret (and they themselves) will remain. It is expressly forbidden to choose the well-being of one intelligent species over another. Yet that's exactly what Kal's parents did, and now the rest of us are doing it, too. I'm fairly certain Dad's pretending not to know anything in order to protect everyone involved and because he secretly likes humans, too. The first time I saw him at dinner following BEAST, I got a vague mumble of "I'm proud of you, son" when he passed by my chair. That's good enough for me.

Kal has only been able to reach us once since that time at the statue. Annika and I were with Aunt Rae in her kitchen when he found us. It was the first time Aunt Rae got to talk to any of them, so, needless to say, she was very happy and we got extra helpings of cherry pie later. Annika asked Kal's parents—or the Sheinblatts as she still insists on calling them—why they wanted to save Earth so badly that they'd risk so much for it.

"Well, Annika, it was your dad's chili cheese fries," Kal's father had admitted. "They were just delightful. Couldn't let the Niffum take those away from humanity."

At the mention of her dad and his fries, Annika's eyes got bright red, and she didn't ask anything else after that.

"And the soap operas!" Kal's mother had added sheepishly. Aunt Rae laughed, but this made no sense to me. We have plenty of soap here in The Realms and who likes opera, anyway? Whatever their real reasons, I'm glad they did it, and I'm doing what I can to protect their secret. We haven't heard from Kal since then, though, and I try not to dwell on what that might mean.

"C'mon, Joss," Annika says, tugging on my arm and basically hauling me into a standing position. "I want to get to the view screens before the other kids get there today. The Niffum are getting closer and closer to where Earth used to be."

I grumble and look around the room for my holoscreen. I always lose that thing, which drives Annika crazy. She keeps sending me texts on it that I don't answer. I told her she needs to get with the program and use the hologram feature, but she says no one needs to see a 3-D image of her asking, *"When are you getting home from delivering those pies already so we can go bowling?"*

I find the holoscreen under a pile of comics and stuff it into my pocket.

"And it wouldn't hurt you to change your clothes," Annika adds. "I'm getting really tired of seeing you in that outfit."

I look down at my clothes. I never give them a second thought. When you're a kid, clothes in The Realms are purely functional. Colorless and nondescript, mostly. I glare at her. "I really need to get a lock on my door."

"Haven't you noticed your brothers have started dressing better since I've gotten here?" she asks.

I shake my head. Although now that she mentions it, both Bren and Grayden *have* looked a little more colorful lately. A splash of blue around the collar, a touch of red on the tips of their shoes. But all I say is, "Guys don't notice what other guys wear." If I truly had to be honest, she's influenced more than just what people wear around here. If it wasn't for her, I'd never have known being the seventh son actually did come with some extra benefits, and some extra responsibilities, which I'm still trying to sort out.

Even with me sleeping in, we still manage to be the first to arrive at school. Annika's right, the Niffum have now reached the outskirts of the Milky Way. They are only a few thousand light-years away now, approaching the spiral arm where the solar system used to be. It won't be long. In the time we've been secretly tracking them, we've seen them briefly orbit eleven other planets and move on without finding what they needed there. Kal explained to us that the Niffum fleet can only travel their preset course, so once they've passed through the spot where they would expect to find Earth, they'll have no choice but to keep going. Once that happens, we'll be able to try getting everyone back again.

Annika and I watch the fleet move silently through space until the teacher calls us away. I take out my holoscreen, ready to take notes. I've been paying more attention in school lately, which I can't blame on Annika, although I'd like to. After everything that's happened, I'm just trying to learn a little more about the universe, and about the part The Realms play in it.

What I told Annika when I first met her was right. It's not magic, what we do. It's all the rules of nature, set up at the very start of our universe. There's a lot I still don't understand, though, and no one seems willing or able to explain it to me. I don't understand why The Realms are so different from everywhere else in the universe. If Kal's in another universe, how many others are there, and what are they like? How are we able to pull planets and people out of time, and how can we accelerate time to get it back?

Fortunately for me, being the patient person that I am, I can wait to learn the answers. As long as I don't have to wait *too* long.

After school I return with Annika to Aunt Rae's house, always the first stop on my route now. Bren is waiting with a plate of pie and some new game to show her. "Leave the door open," Aunt Rae calls out as the two of them disappear into Annika's room.

I'm not sure why Aunt Rae said that, but I'm kind of glad.

"Only three for today," she says, hefting the steaming pie boxes into my arms. I feel the familiar weight work its way through me when I touch them. Why had I never stopped to wonder why no one else mentioned feeling like that when they touched a pie? It's like I've been woken up when I didn't even know I was asleep.

"We're almost back on track," Aunt Rae adds, wiping her flour-covered hands on her apron.

Because of everything that's happened, I have a lot of deliveries to make up for. Not only from Aunt Rae, but from the other pie makers, too. I don't mind the extra work, now that I know what my job actually entails. Hey, maybe it's not too late to write that essay!

As soon as I step out the door, I hear the drums. It's been so long that my first thought is that the banging sound is probably just the boys down the street kicking their ball. I'm about to pass through Aunt Rae's front gate when I hear it again. I rest the pies on the ground and strain my ears. Definitely drumbeats! He's still alive!

I turn to go back into the house to get Annika and Bren, but then Annika cheers as one of her video avatars scores a goal or kills an alien or something, and I change my mind. "Kal?" I call out, running to the street instead.

"It's time, Joss," he says, or rather, his disembodied voice does.

"Time?" I repeat.

"I know the word is unfamiliar to you."

"Hey, I'm getting better. Sort of."

"Tell the others, okay?" His voice takes on an urgency I haven't heard since his first contact. "The Niffum fleet is nearing where the solar system used to be. Once they're past, you'll need to get to work. I'd start now."

"Hey, that's great!" I say, trying to sound like I mean it. And I do mean it. Of course I mean it.

Don't I?

I clear my throat. "I'll gather everyone together now."

"Wait, Joss. In case this doesn't work, and, um, I don't get to tell you this... I just want to say... I'm really sorry for all the secrecy, and for having to spoil what you'd worked so hard to do. You know, before. With the box and then when you were making that totally awesome sun. I didn't want to rat out my parents, and I didn't want you to stop trying for Annika's sake. It all just got really confusing."

"You've already apologized, Kal. I get it."

"Okay, okay. I'll still owe you a big one when you get me back."

"I'll hold you to that."

His voice breaks a little. "Hurry, Joss. Okay?"

That's the first time he's ever sounded openly desperate.

I nod. "Hang in there." Not that I know if there's actually anything to hang on to. He's never described where he is.

I've been picturing this black void of nothingness, with them sort of floating in the air, but for all I know they could have been lounging on beach chairs overlooking paradise. Probably not, though.

As I run back into the house, I force myself to push aside the cold, hard truth. In order to get Kal and his parents back and restore the inhabitants of Earth and the Afterlives, not to mention the rest of the solar system, I will have to give up something I've grown very used to having around.

I wonder if she'll miss me, too.

24

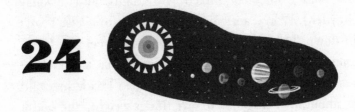

We gather around the still-scorched spot of land where my sun had its short, blazing run at glory. Annika has been unusually quiet since I told her the news from Kal. I think she's afraid to get her hopes up again. I don't blame her. Since recovering the data dots, I've watched the films over and over again. I'm as prepared as I'm ever going to be.

I still don't understand how we're going to be make five billion years of history pass as though it weren't any time at all. My mother tried to explain it to me on the way here, but the whole sixth-smartest-out-of-seven thing kicked in, and I stopped following after a while. Basically it's something about space and time actually being two parts of a whole, which I knew, and you simply have to know how to manipulate space in order to manipulate time, which I didn't know. Bottom line is, it's something we can do here in The Realms and I might as well accept it.

Everyone watches me now, their faces reflecting a wide range of emotions—pride (Mom, Thade, and Aunt Rae), excitement (Bren), excitement mixed with doubt (Ty, Ash, Laz), and excitement mixed with doubt and jealousy (Grayden). Worry, anticipation, and something else I can't pin down flash across Annika's pinched face. She keeps yanking tiny pieces off the leaves on her hat and flicking them onto the ground. She knows what Thade had told me, about my being able to give things weight. She said it sounded like I can control a particle called a Higgs boson, which scientists on Earth had only recently discovered. So really, she knew about all this before I did.

"Here goes," I say, closing my eyes and picturing an invisible field all around me, filled with these tiny particles that turn nothing into something when they come in contact. I instantly feel a current move through me, and I can tell things are happening. I'm not making them happen, not exactly. It's not happening because of me. It's happening *with* me. There's a difference. And I'm not the only one. I can feel, even without seeing, that my brothers have joined me. We are links in some unseen but very real cosmic chain.

I know I'm not supposed to stare into the sun, but I can't help taking a peek. The scene before me is hard to sort out at first. Everything is unfolding so rapidly, like random playing cards being shuffled and somehow ending up in exactly the right order. I can see the sun expanding and brightening so quickly that I know this will be a much, much bigger thing than the sun I had made before. Hydrogen fuses into helium so fast, so violently, that the helium then creates carbon and oxygen. Now comes neon, sodium, magnesium, sulfur, and silicon. And more and more, until the core is filled with iron. And then I can feel a change. The giant, massive star collapses in upon itself, and then instantly explodes in a shock wave that knocks all of us to the ground. We scramble to our feet as gold and silver and lead spew forth into the gas and atoms that already fill this place. And then...a new sun is born! Smaller this time, and much more stable. The dust and rocks left over start to come together into larger and larger spheres.

And before I know it, the baby planets are back! Some of rock, some of gas. All spinning, all bombarded over and over and over again by large asteroids and smaller comets and meteorites carrying water and amino acids. The huge gas planets get pushed far away from the sun, some turning onto their sides where they will remain forever lopsided. The largest of the rocky ones settles into its not-quite-circular orbit. Earth is back in place!

Barren and empty, the imperfect sphere is suddenly struck by a chunk of rock so large it shears the top layer off the planet and sends it whirling into space. I know time is passing, but before I can blink, the pieces have come together. Earth has a moon!

Volcanoes and earthquakes shake the planet, and before long, oceans boil from the heat of it. If anything goes wrong, at any step of the way, we'll have failed. None of us move as we watch the ground and oceans of the new Earth cool. When the conditions are just right, the seeds of life sprout, slowly filling the air with oxygen. Creatures swim and crawl and run and dance. Millions of species, adapting to their environments, changing and surviving. Consciousness arrives, then self-awareness. Humans begin to communicate with language, form communities, make decisions and art, and grow food. They begin to wonder at their own existence.

I cannot look away as in droves, they leave the caves and huts, claw their way toward understanding, try and fail and try again, relentlessly, to get smarter, faster, farther, better. I see flashes of faces flickering by me, links on one family's chain, altering slightly with each generation until...Annika?

Annika! I whirl around so fast I fall to the ground again. She is not here. Where is she? She was right behind me when I closed my eyes! How long ago was that? A few minutes? A few billion years? It all feels the same. No one else notices my panic. They're all smiling and high-fiving each other, which Annika taught us and in which my brothers take a seemingly endless amount of joy, high-fiving each other at any given opportunity.

Bren runs over to me and yanks me up. He puts up his hand to high-five. When I don't move, he lifts my hand up for me and pushes it against his.

"Where's Annika?" My voice is hoarse, like it hasn't been used in a long time. "Have you seen her?"

But he's not listening. He's pointing into the field. "Look, Joss!" His voice sounds as creaky as mine. "How cool is that?"

Impatient, I look out to see the sun is far, far away now, a gum ball–size dot in the blackness of space. Much closer, a medium-size, slightly tilted blue-green planet slowly rotates. As we watch, everything sinks down, like a curtain call at the end of a show. The gum ball sun, the blue-green planet Earth, the dusty Mars, the fiery Jupiter, all of them go down, out of The Realms, to take their rightful places in the distant Milky Way far beneath our feet.

Mom appears beside me and squeezes my hand. "It's magnificent. I have a feeling you'll ace Planet Building class next term."

"Mom, where's Annika? What happened?"

She doesn't let go of my hand. I'm pretty sure I know what she's about to say, but maybe I'm wrong. Maybe Annika merely had to go to the bathroom. Humans have to do that a lot. It's pretty disturbing.

"Annika's gone," Mom says.

I hunch forward a bit, like someone just punched me in the stomach. I know this was the outcome we'd hoped for, but I hadn't really thought it through. I think a part of me still hadn't believed it would work.

"I know it's hard to lose a friend," Mom says, "and you've certainly had more than your fair share of that lately. But look. This will make you feel better." She turns me around.

The Universe has shouted itself alive. We are one of the shouts.
                                        —**Ray Bradbury, writer**

25

When I squint, I can see two hazy figures running toward us from the right, and one lone figure from the left. They're moving fast and getting closer and my eyes get sharper, and then…"Kal!" I shout, running toward the lone figure. I consider turning my legs into wheels, but I'm still pulling out pieces of dirt from when I chased after Bren. I found a button behind my left ankle only a little while ago.

"Joss!" Kal yells. "Joss! I'm back! You did it!"

I want to tell him that I didn't really do much of anything. It all just…happened. But for now I'm too glad to see him to argue. I keep running. My brothers and Mom and Aunt Rae run alongside me. Ty breaks off toward the Afterlives. Now that all the residents from Earth are back, he's going to have his hands full sorting it all out.

We all meet up in the middle, shouting and whooping

and high-fiving, even the grown-ups. Seeing Kal again makes everything that happened seem unreal, like something I dreamed. Even though I don't dream.

Kal's mother pulls me aside.

"Annika is back where she belongs, Joss. Her family didn't even know she'd gone. No one even knows *they'd* gone!"

Relief floods through me. I didn't realize how scared I was that she'd just disappeared, maybe to an Earth that didn't bare any resemblance to the one she left, no matter how carefully I'd reviewed the holofilms. "You actually saw her there?"

She nods. "Kal's father and I were pulled back to Earth, just as we'd hoped. We ran over to Annika's house, not sure what we'd find. But we knew she must have done her job and not looked in the telescope. We wouldn't have gotten back otherwise."

"But was she okay? What did she say to you?"

"She couldn't really say much. She wasn't supposed to know us as anything other than her parents' friends from down the street. Anyway, she was too busy hugging her parents and swinging her brother around to bother with anyone else. Before we took the wormhole back here, we made sure the coordinates of The Realms were deleted from their telescope."

"Thanks for letting me know," I tell her, even as I feel a twinge in my stomach. I'm grateful that Annika's safe and happy and that everything seems to have worked out. But it feels weird not to be able to celebrate with her. I feel a little like I did when Kal disappeared, like something important is missing inside me. But then Kal starts telling everyone about how he materialized right in the middle of PTB headquarters, and I focus on that and how happy I am that he's back.

"You should have seen your dad, Joss!" Kal says, grinning. "It was classic! He was sitting at his desk when I showed up in the middle of his office. He jumped so high he banged his legs on the bottom of the desk really hard! I said, 'Ouch, that's gonna leave a mark,' and he said things like, 'Where did you—' and 'How did you—' and then 'I'm glad you're back.' It took me being sucked into another universe in order for your dad to say something nice to me!"

Kal's dad turns to Mom. "You'll have to forgive my son. He's just overly excited. He means no disrespect toward your husband."

"No, ma'am, I don't," Kal says.

"I know," Mom says, clasping Kal's hand. "And I'm glad you're back, too."

"Oh!" Kal's mom suddenly says to me, reaching into her pocket. "I almost forgot! Annika gave me this for you."

My hand closes around a stiff, folded piece of paper. There's no way I'm opening it with all these curious eyes on me.

"What is it?" Kal asks. "A present? Did I miss your birthday?"

To my relief, Mom claps her hands for everyone's

attention, and I give a little apologetic shrug to Kal and turn to listen. "The Powers That Be are going to have a lot of questions about what happened here," she says. "Direct them to me. I'll handle the fallout."

Kal's dad reaches for my mom's arm. "Are you sure? We don't want to cause trouble for you."

She smiles warmly. "I'm sure. Being married to the Supreme Overlord has some perks."

The walk back to the central Realms is leisurely, much more like the way things used to be. I'm surprised how quickly I relax into the rhythm of it. Nowhere to rush to, nothing to worry about. My brothers pepper Kal with questions about what his universe was like. I listen to him describe how he and his parents were pretty much stranded in this void of darkness (I was right!), where particles of matter and antimatter kept annihilating each other in flashes of light. Unlike our own universe, it became too dense and started to collapse. My mind keeps coming back to the little folded paper in my pocket.

We all eventually split off into different directions. Mom and Kal's parents to PTB headquarters, my brothers to their jobs, and Kal and I to Aunt Rae's.

"I can't wait to get home," Kal admits. "Remind me never to complain about being bored again."

"You never really do."

He grins. "True! I always have you and my music to keep me entertained."

I cringe. As much as I missed Kal, I sure didn't miss his

music. I bet Aunt Rae's thinking about how she can unfix her hearing again. She immediately ushers Kal into the kitchen and plies him with food and pie. I give them some privacy to catch up, and head down the hall to Annika's room. I mean, Kal's room. This is all going to take some getting used to.

I push the door open slowly, half-expecting to still see Annika's pink walls and vision board. But no. Kal's room is just as I remember seeing it last. Bed unmade, electronics covering every surface except for the ones already covered in comic books. Seeing it like this only makes it harder to believe that it was ever anything different.

I take the note out of my pocket and sit down on the bed. I've never gotten a note from a girl before. Well, I've never gotten a note period.

I unfold it and am surprised when two small objects fall out of the otherwise blank paper. I pick up the shiny gold chain first and watch it shimmer against my palm. Annika's grandmother's bracelet. I can't believe she gave it to me. I put it in my pocket for safekeeping. I'm going to take really good care of it. Much better than my holoscreen.

The other thing that fell out looks like a circular piece of metal, like a gigantic data dot, but with a small hole in the middle. I turn it over in my hand. A piece of human technology, certainly. But what's on it? No place like Kal's room to find out!

I try slipping the disc into one machine after another. Mostly it doesn't fit, or the machine blinks out an error message. Finally I find one that makes a whirring sound when the disc is inserted. The dark screen suddenly lights up with Annika's face. She's sitting on her bed in her pink room and at first I'm confused. How could she have filmed this here? I don't think she had a video camera with her. Then I realize that of course she didn't. Her bedroom is back home with her. Or rather, she's back home in her bedroom.

"Hi, Joss!" she says cheerily. "Sagan and I have something to say." She leans over and picks up a huge black-and-white cat. "Sagan, say hi to my friend Joss."

My stomach flutters a bit, which is kind of embarrassing. She takes the cat's paw and waves it at me. I find myself waving back, which is even more embarrassing.

She puts down Sagan, who meows and scampers away. "Oh well," she says. "I guess he didn't miss me as much as I missed him. It's so weird being back here, just like I never left. My parents and my brother don't seem to realize anything happened at all. Isn't that amazing?" She shakes her head with the wonder of it all. "Hey, notice anything different about me? No leaves in my hair. Yay!"

I smile. She looks kind of different without them. Younger, but older, too, if that makes sense. It probably doesn't.

"I was going to write you a real letter," she continues, "but I knew you'd make fun of me for being so old-fashioned. So this is as close as I can come to sending a hologram. Anyway, I only have a minute because I know

Kal's parents are anxious to hop in that wormhole thingy and get back to The Realms." She laughs. "Boy, those words sound weird! You don't have to worry about me ever telling anyone about you because they'll think I've gone totally insane." Then she pauses for a minute, thoughtful. "I think I want to keep it all to myself, anyway. Did you know Kal's parents used the information on humans that they took from Gluck to reconfigure the wormhole just for me?"

So *that* was the big project they were working on! I wonder how long they'd been planning this!

"If they hadn't sent me to The Realms, I would have gotten pulled out of time with everyone else and there wouldn't have been anyone to, you know, represent Earth. And, well, I never would have met a boy with weird hair, perfect skin, and a really nice smile. I'm talking about you, in case you didn't pick that up."

She likes my smile?

A knock on the door causes her to jump. "Just a second, Mom."

"Go to bed, hon. Tomorrow's a school day."

"I will," she calls out. "I'm just finishing something up."

Hearing her mom's voice flashes me back to the holoscreen image of a happy, laughing woman. Annika must have missed her more than she let on. She must have missed everything more than she let on.

"I've got to go, Joss. Promise me you'll visit Grandpa and

the real Sagan in the Afterlives and tell them I'm okay. And thank the professor for all his help, okay? I'm only reminding you to do this because you're a boy and manners aren't your strong suit."

"They weren't yours, either," I remind her, then realize I'm talking to myself. I hope Kal didn't hear that.

"Being in The Realms was an amazing adventure," she says, blinking quickly. "I'll obviously never forget it. Thank you for always looking out for me. And for..." Now she gives up on the blinking and just starts crying. "And for giving me my family back. And...please thank the Sheinblatts—I mean, Kal's parents—for saving all of us in the first place and for giving Earth a second chance. I hope the Niffum find another planet they can live on." She sniffs and wipes at her eyes. "When things get hard or sad or whatever, it'll make me feel really safe to know you're out there." She waves her arms around her room. "Somewhere. I was never really clear on where, exactly, you are."

I feel a burning behind my eyes. This is the closest I've come to crying myself. If I actually had tear ducts, I'm sure I would be. And I wouldn't even care who saw.

"Okay," she continues, "now that I probably look terrible, I better say good-bye. Study hard in school, and I bet in no time you'll be the *fifth*-smartest brother, at least! Now that I'll never have to find out what would happen if I turned my back on a Niffum in the rain, I've come up with a new catchphrase. Or, you know, a bit of advice for any

future humans who find themselves stuck in The Realms."
She smooths down her hair and says, "Never turn your
back on the seventh son of the Supreme Overlord of the
Universe...unless you want a bucket of water thrown on
your head."

She winks, leans over, and switches off the camera.

There are only two ways to live your life. One is as though nothing is a miracle. The other is as though everything is a miracle.

—**Albert Einstein, physicist**

26

Sometimes Bren comes with me to visit her, sometimes Kal. But usually I'm alone. I like to go after my delivery route. Occasionally I'll bring an extra slice of pie with me, but only if Aunt Rae made cherry, because that was Annika's favorite.

It's a long walk to the Hall of Species, but I don't mind. Mom understands if I'm late to dinner on these days. I use the extra key Ash finally agreed to give me, and let myself in. As usual, I'm the only one here.

I spread out my picnic blanket in front of Annika's holostatue (which Ash set up right between the three-eyed Zolta and a feathery Pollyphemus) and unpack my bagel with cream cheese and Red Hots. I don't know if she still eats them, of course, since it's been more than seventy years Earth time since I saw her, but I've found a supplier and developed a taste for them.

I've had some good adventures since the day Ash took this 3-D holo-image of her, but none as good as the ones we had together. Dad finally admitted that I hadn't been allowed to leave The Realms before because they thought my having some kind of connection with gravity might cause damage to the sun of whatever planet I was visiting. Had they just TOLD me I had this connection, I could have learned to control it, as I eventually did. I've since visited three planets (never Earth, though) and managed not to blow up any suns during my stay.

The last time I played Annika's video I couldn't help but wonder how many of the goals on her vision board she'd achieved. After that, I stopped watching it. I've also never used the video screens at school to check on her, or even asked Kal's parents for any updates when they visited Earth. Every once in a while they'll let slip that they saw her, but I always cover my ears. I want to respect her privacy, but I also kind of don't want to know what she's doing. It's very strange to think how much of her life span she's lived since she left The Realms, and not much has changed for me. I may be slightly taller, and hopefully more than slightly wiser, and my bowling score has improved, but that's about it. She would have grown up, had a career, had adventures. Did she get married? Have a family? It hurts to think about it.

The communication network buzzes, and I jump. My bagel goes flying and winds up cream-cheese-side down in front of the Zolta, who, if he were alive, would no doubt have snatched it up already.

"Joss!" The voice fills the cavernous room. "Are you there?"

I reach for the bagel and brush it off. "Kal?"

"Why don't you have your holoscreen? I've been looking everywhere for you."

I pat my empty pockets. I still can't manage to keep track of that thing. "Kal, unless you're trapped in another universe again, can you come talk to me in person? The com system is only for emergencies."

"This IS an emergency! That's what I'm trying to tell you."

"Oh. What is it, then?" I can't get myself too worked up. Kal thinks it's an emergency when one of his drumsticks rolls under the drum set and he has to stop mid-banging to pick it up.

"She's here," he says.

I pick up a stray Red Hot from the floor and push it back onto the bagel. I figure the floors are pretty clean, since not many people come here and the small cinnamon candy is a valuable item. "Who's where?" I ask.

"Annika! She just arrived at the Afterlives, so get your butt down here!"

The bagel goes flying once again. I leave everything behind and run out of the building so fast I don't even remember standing up. I instantly turn my legs into wheels.

I don't even care about what I'll have to pull out of them later. All that matters is getting there as fast as possible.

Deep down, I knew this day would come. I had tried to push it out of my mind. On one hand, it will mean Annika and I get to see each other again. But on the other hand, if she's in the Afterlives, that means she's dead, and a dead Annika is something I can't even consider. But now I no longer have the luxury of denial.

The reflecting walls of the Afterlives loom in the distance, although I'm still far away. I had gone back there as requested, to give Annika's messages to her grandfather and Professor Sagan. Annika's grandfather was so happy he cried, which was awkward, what with the whole "no crying in the Afterlives" thing. And the professor was utterly amazed—and grateful—that we'd pulled it off. I have avoided going back, though. The dead should have their privacy.

Both Ty and Kal meet me at the main entrance to the huge structure. The two of them share a glance that I don't like the looks of, and lead me over to a bench, which, like most things in The Realms, is more of a wispy *suggestion* of a bench. "Sit," Ty commands.

"What's going on? Is Annika . . . okay? I mean, I can't believe she's . . . she's . . ." I can't even make myself say the word.

Ty finishes the sentence for me. "Can't believe she's dead."

I swallow hard and nod.

"Well, you don't have to worry," Kal says. "Because she's not."

I jump off the bench. "What? You said she was here. I don't understand. Ty?"

Ty puts out his hand to calm me down. "She *is* here. Well, she *was* here. She just isn't dead."

I turn to Kal. "Did you see her come into the Afterlives or not?"

He shakes his head. "She snuck by me."

"How? Isn't it your job to escort everyone?"

He shrugs sheepishly. "She's got skills, that one."

I turn back to Ty. "Explain. Please, Ty. How can she be here and not here, dead and not dead?"

Ty tugs at his collar. Mom should really get him looser shirts. "Well, it's complicated. This has never happened before."

Kal cuts in. "The chick escaped. She tricked us, then escaped. Man, you'd think an old lady wouldn't be so light on her toes."

"*Escaped?*" I repeat. "From the *Afterlives*?"

Ty reddens. "Okay, so as far as we can piece it together, Annika used the same wormhole Kal's parents set up OnWorld all those years ago. She must have been guarding it carefully, or she had some help." He throws a suspicious glance Kal's way.

Kal holds up his hands. "Hey, don't look at me. I'm not my parents' keeper."

"Anyway," Ty continues, clearly unconvinced, "somehow she took the wormhole back here, snuck into the Afterlives when neither Kal nor I was on duty, then she tricked Trib, a perfectly decent fellow in my department, into starting a sim for her."

I listen to his story with disbelief. I'm trying to picture an eighty-three-year-old version of Annika doing all this. It's impossible to picture. "Then what?"

"Well, you know how we always check in on the newbies?"

I shake my head.

"Well, we do. Trib went in to her sim to make sure everything was running smoothly, and then she followed him right out! No one's ever done that before. They've wandered accidentally, as you know, but never on purpose."

I can't help but smile. That's because no one ever knew they were in a simulation before. "Why would she do that?" I ask. "Where is she now?"

"I have a feeling I know the answer to *why*," Ty grumbles. "As to where she went, that's anyone's guess."

"I know why, too," Kal says. "She did it for you, Joss. The sim she chose was from the day she first came here. Breaking out in the middle of that one was the only way to get her youth back." He shakes his head in admiration. "A live human, turning back her own clock by manipulating the system. Man, she's good."

I feel my pulse speed up. "I've got to go."

"Do you want me to come with you?" Kal asks.

"No, but thank you for everything!" I take off running toward the central Realms.

"I didn't do anything!" he calls after me. But he did. Kal's always been there for me, always been someone I can trust. Friends like that come around once in a lifetime. Or, if I'm lucky enough, twice.

I hear her heartbeats before I even get close. How did that guy Trib miss that sound? As a general rule, people entering the Afterlives do not have beating hearts. That's kind of the point.

I burst into Aunt Rae's kitchen just as Annika puts the last forkful of cherry pie into her mouth. She swallows and grins, pieces of cherry dotting her teeth. "Oh, hey, Joss," she says, as though it's the most normal thing in the world to find her here, eating pie, looking exactly the same as I remember her. Exactly like her holostatue in the Hall of Species.

"Hey, Annika," I reply.

"Do I have pie in my teeth?"

I grin. "Yes. Yes, you do."

She pushes back her chair. "Let's go for a walk."

So we do. We go for a walk. And it feels utterly, totally normal and right.

She points at my feet. "Your boots have color. And a pattern."

I grin again. Or maybe I just haven't stopped. "An old friend once told me I needed to brighten up my wardrobe. I'm also an inch taller."

"So you are." We keep walking.

"It's a good thing you never dated my friend Lydia after all," she says, as though it were ever really an option. "Remember how she used to like guys with weird haircuts?"

I nod, unable to stop looking at her.

"Well, then she grew up and stopped being cool and started playing bridge all the time and told boring stories about her boring kids and her even more boring grandkids. You would have been totally bored."

"Wow," I say. "Really dodged a bullet there, didn't I?"

"Sure did," she says.

Neither of us speaks for a minute, and our steps get very small. Finally, I say, "So. Pretty sneaky, what you did back there at the Afterlives. Unbelievable, really."

"Yeah. That was something."

"One for the history books."

"I suspect so."

"And figuring out how to use that wormhole. Bet it took a lot of planning."

"You could say that."

We look at each other's faces for a while. "Hey, you don't have your leaf hat on."

"I know," she says, feeling the top of her bare head. "I don't need it now. I think it has to do with breaking out of the sim, where I could breathe. Or maybe because I shut down the wormhole once I got here, making me an official resident of The Realms now. Either way, I'm not complaining."

"Maybe I should be prepared with a bucket of water just in case."

She laughs.

"Annika?"

"Yes?"

I reach for her hand. "I'm really, really glad you did this."

"Softish," she says, squeezing my hand. "Just like I remember."

"Welcome home."

"Thanks."

We stand there like that for a long, long time. There's so much I want to tell her, so much I want to ask about her life. But it can wait. Time is long here. And we've got a lot of it.

"Joss?" she says. "Can I ask you something?"

"Anything."

She points at my left leg. "Is that a Red Hot stuck to your knee?"

Author's Note

We are in the universe, and the universe is in us.
—Neil deGrasse Tyson, astronomer

Yes, even the Author's Note gets a quote at the beginning! Dr. Tyson's words sum up one of the underlying themes of *Pi in the Sky*. We live in the universe; that's something we take for granted. Of course we live in it. But it lives in us just as much. Our very atoms are a part of the fabric of the cosmos, cooked inside stars that exploded billions of years ago. We are the universe made conscious. This is something I never truly grasped until I started doing research for this book and began to truly understand how we, and all living things, fit into the larger picture.

Building a fictional story around the latest discoveries in science was a challenging and rewarding experience. Technology continues to offer unprecedented access into the universe, and people working in fields like astronomy, cosmology, astrophysics, and astrobiology are discovering new and incredible things every day. How can you find out more? Check out space.com or nasa.gov, and get a daily e-mail about the most exciting discoveries of the day by signing up at dailygalaxy.com. Two books I love, both geared for young readers, are *The Magic of Reality* by Richard Dawkins (also an awesome app) and *A Really Short History of Nearly Everything* by Bill Bryson. I also recommend interactive science apps like *Brian Cox's Wonders of the Universe*, *Star Walk*, and *The Elements: A Visual Exploration* from Theodore Gray. So much information at our fingertips. It is an exciting time to be alive.

I want to thank the brilliant scientists and writers whose insights open each chapter of *Pi in the Sky* and give the book its shape and structure. The plotline was originally inspired by a class of sixth graders at Park Middle School in New Jersey. They had read my book *Every Soul a Star* and put together a bunch of quotes they thought I would like. One of them, from Carl Sagan, grabbed me at once: "To make an apple pie from scratch, you must first invent the universe." I knew what he was saying, about how the elements inside the pie—and inside everything—came from the birth of the universe, but I kept thinking of other ways to interpret it. What if I turned it around? What if there was someone out there actually using a pie to create the universe? And what would happen if someone on Earth found out?

As I began my research, two quotes jumped out at me. The first was from physicist Paul Davies: "Dark matter holds the key to the universe." The second was from mathematical physicist Edward Witten: "We don't know what the dark matter is made of, but there is a very interesting theory that it consists of exotic elementary particles that are part of the cosmic rays." Together, these statements gave me the idea to set the story "inside" dark matter, which I'm pretty sure doesn't actually HAVE an inside. At least not with people living in it. But hey, you never know. Personally, I think we've only started to glimpse the supreme weirdness of the universe. Or multiverse. Or whatever this wacky place we call home actually is.

And thus, the idea for *Pi in the Sky* was born.

Funny story about the title. When I first started working on the story, a few young readers suggested I title it *Pie in the Sky*, which I thought was a clever play on words, both because there really WAS a pie in the sky in the story, and also because the phrase means "an idea or scheme that is utterly impractical or unlikely," which applied so nicely to the task that lay ahead for the main characters in the story. Anyway, I was telling my father-in-law the plotline, and when I got to the title, he couldn't hear me very well and asked, "P-i-e like the kind you eat, or p-i like the math equation?" And suddenly I knew it had to be pi, the ratio of a circle's circumference to its diameter. Something that you can't measure the planets, or the distances between them, or their orbits, without.

Okay, so maybe that story wasn't fall-on-the-floor funny, or maybe you just had to be there (on a curb at a noisy street fair). Anyway, thanks, Steve!

I am very grateful to the young readers who gave me

advice on the first draft and to the scientists (many—but not all—from my own family!) who answered my questions along the way and who double-checked my facts afterward: Jeremy Kahn, mathematician; Jennifer Mass, chemist; Steven Brawer, physicist; Adam Finnefrock, physicist; and Elan Grossman, astronomer and neuroscientist, who gets bonus points for answering e-mails at three a.m., no matter how ridiculous my questions were. Thank you to astronomer and astrophysicist Gregory Laughlin for allowing me to paraphrase his words in the fictional Carl Sagan's speech at the end of chapter 15. A special thank-you to my editor, Alvina Ling, and her always insightful partner in crime Bethany Strout for never pointing out that if I spent less time watching television documentaries about the universe and more time writing, this book would have been done a lot sooner.

The world lost one of its brightest literary lights as this book was nearing completion. I want to pay homage to the masterful Ray Bradbury, whose imagination, wisdom, humor, and sense of wonder and joy shone through every line he wrote. I hope he found something really cool on the other side.

The best writing makes you look at the world differently. It celebrates life, and the miracle of it. Bradbury's stories do that. The following passages do that, too, by opening a window to a new way of looking at our existence.

Every living thing is, from the cosmic perspective, incredibly lucky simply to be alive. Most, 90 percent and more, of all the organisms that have ever lived have died without viable offspring, but not a single one of your ancestors, going back to the dawn of life on Earth, suffered that normal misfortune. You spring from an unbroken line of winners going back billions of generations, and those winners were, in every generation, the luckiest of the lucky, one out of a hundred or a thousand or even a million.

—Daniel C. Dennett, philosopher,
Freedom Evolves

After sleeping through a hundred million centuries we have finally opened our eyes on a sumptuous planet, sparkling with color, bountiful with life. Within decades we must close our eyes again. Isn't it a noble, an enlightened way of spending our brief time in the sun, to work at understanding the universe and how we have come to wake up in it?

—Richard Dawkins, biologist,
Unweaving the Rainbow

Last but not least, here's a neat trick if you have nothing to do after school one day. Disconnect your cable TV and scan for a channel you can't receive. That static you see hopping and jumping on the screen? A small percentage of it is the afterglow from the big bang. How can you be bored watching the birth of the universe?

Thank you so much for reading. Please remember, you are stronger than you think. You are made of the same stuff as stars, and you shine just as bright. Many blessings upon your head.

Peace,
Wendy

P.S. You haven't tried bagels with cream cheese and Red Hots? Soooo good.

Reader's Guide

1. What job does Joss have? How is it different from his brothers' jobs? How does Joss feel about his role?

2. Do you think Joss has a positive self-image?

3. When Joss first meets Annika, what is his impression of her? Use specific details to support your answer.

4. Why is it important for Annika to believe that she is dreaming? What information does Gluck provide that supports this?

5. What is the relationship like between Joss and his brother Ty? What does Ty do when Annika is pulled through the wall? What does Ty's reaction show about his personality?

6. What is Annika's reaction when Joss refers to humans as "primitive"? Based on his explanation, in what ways is Earth primitive? In what ways is it advanced? Annika offers several examples to try to convince Joss that humans are not primitive. What examples would you use?

7. Carl Sagan tells Joss that Earth is worth saving. What reasons does he give? Do you think he makes a good argument? How are his reasons different from the ones Annika gave earlier?

8. Why does Joss want to discover which chemicals are in Annika's body? What does Ash suggest is the best way to collect these samples? What does Annika think of that idea?

9. Why does Bren take the data dots and sabotage the formation of the sun? Do you think Joss will forgive his brother? Why or why not?

10. In what ways has Annika helped people in The Realms change? How has she helped Joss?

11. What does Joss have to give up in order to get Kal back and restore Earth and its solar system? How do you think this decision will affect Joss's life?

12. Why, do you think, does Joss try to avoid hearing updates about Annika? Why does he say, "It hurts to think about it"? What does he mean?

If you liked

**don't miss another
great novel by
wendy mass!**

Available now

Turn the page for a sneak peek!

ALLY

1

In Iceland, fairies live inside of rocks. Seriously. They have houses in there and schools and amusement parks and everything.

Besides me, not many people outside of Iceland know this. But you just have to read the right books and it's all there. When you're homeschooled, you have a lot of books. I also know how to find every constellation in the sky, and that the brightest star in any constellation is called the Alpha. I know all the constellations because my father taught them to me, and I know about the Alpha because it is also my name. But my family and friends call me Ally.

Okay, that's not entirely true. I don't really have any friends. Not within hundreds of miles, anyway. And it's not because I am unlikable or smell bad or anything like that. In fact, I take a bath every single day in the hot spring outside our house, and everyone knows that the minerals in hot springs make you smell like fresh air all day long.

The fact that we live somewhere with a hot spring outside our house pretty much explains why I don't have friends nearby. Basically, my house is as close to the middle of nowhere as a person can get and still be *somewhere*. Our town is not even on the map. It's not even a town. It's more of an *area*. There's the Moon Shadow Campground that my family owns, where I know every tree and every rock and which foxes are friendly and which aren't, and a tiny general store a mile away, where most everything expired in the last millennium. That's it. The nearest real town is an hour away. Sure, maybe it gets lonely every now and then, but I love it here. I was only four when we moved, so I don't really remember life in civilization, which is what my ten-year-old brother, Kenny, calls anywhere other than here.

It should be pointed out that Kenny's only knowledge of civilization besides our books is based on what he can glean from the ancient black-and-white television at the general store, and since the only show that comes in is the soap opera *Days of Our Lives,* he thinks civilization is very dramatic. And until a few years ago, he thought it was in black-and-white.

Some people might think my parents are crazy for doing what they did — up and leaving their jobs to build a campground in the Middle of Nowhere, USA. But they had a plan. They knew that a decade later, hundreds, maybe thousands of people would travel to this exact spot to be a part of something that hasn't happened in mainland America for over seventy-five years and won't happen again for a hundred more. And this flock, this *throng* of people, would need a comfortable, safe place to stay, wouldn't they? With hot springs and hot coffee and clean bathrooms and their choice of tents or cabins, and no televisions to remind them of anywhere other than here.

My parents knew that, for one day, our two-square-mile campground would be the only patch of land in the entire country to lie smack dab in the path of the Great Eclipse when it passes overhead. In precisely twenty-two days and some hours from now, the sun will get erased from the sky, the planets will come out to greet us, the birds will stop singing, and a glowing halo of light will flutter like angels' wings above our heads.

Except, of course, if it rains.

☽

BREE

1

I was switched at birth.

There's no other explanation for how I wound up in this family. My physicist parents are certified geniuses with, like, a zillion IQ between them and all these grants to study things like dark matter and anti-matter, which are apparently very different things. My eleven-year-old sister Melanie gets straight A's, does cartwheels in public, and actually enjoys watching science documentaries on PBS with my parents. I prefer MTV to PBS, and to me, dark matter and anti-matter really means *don't matter.* But as smart as they are, my family members are all rather plain-looking. Not ugly or anything even close, but just sort of plain. Average. Like soft-serve vanilla ice cream in a cup, not even a cone.

I am not plain or average or — god forbid — vanilla. I am peanut butter rocky road with multicolored sprinkles, hot fudge, and a cherry on top. Not that I would ever EAT such a thing, because it would go right to my thighs.

I don't mean to sound stuck-up, but I happen to be very attractive. My whole life strangers have stopped my mom on the street to say what a beautiful daughter she has. And they aren't talking about Melanie. Granted, you can't help the looks you're born with. I can't help that I'm the tallest girl in my grade, or that I never get pimples, or that my eyes are as blue as Cameron Diaz's. But I make sure to do everything I can to stay beautiful. Every morning I brush my dark brown hair a hundred times until it shines like silk, and if any nails are chipped I fix them with the manicure kit I bought last year at Things of Beauty in the mall. Every night before bed I do fifty sit-ups. I drink bottled water because you only look good on the outside if you're healthy on the inside. My friends and I keep up with all the latest trends, and we share clothes and even shoes sometimes. I worked extremely hard to become one of the most popular girls in my grade, and I work hard at staying there.

Today is the last day of school, and I can't wait for summer. Even though I'm only thirteen and a half, I'm going to be working at Let's Make Up in the mall. I'm only allowed to work two hours a day until I'm fourteen, but that's okay. My official title is "junior consultant" and it's a very important position. When you're a teenager and shopping for a new eyeliner or

☆

lip gloss, you don't want an old lady telling you what you need. You want someone you can identify with. And if a customer happens to think they can look like me just by buying our makeup, then so be it. They buy the makeup, they look better, I get a bonus, and I spend it next door at Hollister. Everybody wins!

My parents, of course, don't see it that way, which harkens back to the whole switched-at-birth theory. They don't understand that while I might not share their goal of discovering what kind of tiny invisible particles the universe is really made of, I still have goals. I plan to work at the mall, get discovered by one of the scouts looking for kids with modeling potential, be on the cover of *Seventeen* BEFORE I'm seventeen, and then make enough money as a supermodel to retire when I'm twenty-five and my beauty is fading. Melanie has accused me of being high-maintenance, but I don't think that's true. I just like things to be orderly and pretty, and I'm happy to give those less fortunate than me tips on how to improve themselves. I like to keep my life uncomplicated. Complicated people get wrinkles before their time.

We all have things to offer the world. My beauty is what I have to give.

And the best thing about being beautiful?

No one (except maybe my deluded parents who don't understand that modeling is a perfectly respectable career choice) expects me to be anything else.

☆

JACK

1

My father has no head.

Well, of course he HAS one, but I've never seen it. All I've seen is about a hundred photos of the rest of his body. A big, roundish guy in suits, shorts, and once even a bear costume. I found the pictures in a shoe box in the back of my mother's closet when I was snooping for Christmas gifts a few years ago. I can just imagine her sitting on the floor of her bedroom, angrily snipping off the heads. I snooped some more in case there was another box with only the heads, but there wasn't. She must have thrown them away.

My mother never talks about my father, who left before I was born. I stopped asking when I realized all it did was make her upset. She said that anyone who would leave his pregnant wife and four-year-old son to go "find himself" didn't deserve another thought. It sure was a terrible thing to do. But it seems to me that my mother is better off alone than with a guy who has no head and ditched his whole family.

Still, I wonder about him. Even in the bear costume, I can tell I inherited his build. Big and wide, and good for one thing only — playing football. And if I was even REMOTELY good at playing football, I'd be all set. But I can't run across the room without getting winded or a cramp in my side. My second-grade gym teacher told me I had two left feet. For a week after that I would only wear left-footed shoes because I thought he meant it literally. My brother Mike has two normal feet, and no problem running across a field. In fact, he's the star first baseman on the high school baseball team. Luckily he's four years older than me, so we won't ever have to be in the same school again. No way can I compete with him in anything. I gave up trying a long time ago. I also gave up trying to pay attention in class. And trying to get people to like me. It's just too much effort. When they look at me, the other kids just see a big pudgy kid who sits in the back of every class drawing in his art book, or on his desk if the teacher confiscated the book. I don't belong to any clubs or after-school activities either. But not paying attention in class came back to bite me on the butt this year. Failing science class gave me a one-way ticket to summer school. It's humiliating. Having to sit in a stifling hot room with a bunch of my fellow rejects learning for the millionth time what the different types of rocks are called. What a total waste of time. All I want to do is be left alone so I can read (fantasy and SF), draw (aliens, monsters, and wizards), and conserve my energy so when everyone else is sleeping and dreaming their normal dreams, I can do something that most other people can't.

I can fly.

A delicious adventure from award-winning author

WENDY MASS

A New York
Times
Bestseller

A sweet and delectable story about four children,
a candy contest, and a mystery that will change their lives forever